INTOXICATING PASSIONS

A COLLECTION OF SEDUCTIVE SHORT STORIES

CHERIL N CLARKE

SWEET DARK RUM

1

I was in a leadership meeting when the flashbacks hit me. The blindfold. The strawberries. The massage oil and the flogger. The stainless-steel pinwheel, fetish feathers, and leather restraints. The scented candles and hot wax, with the steady hum from a spellbinding playlist. We had been at it for hours. The hair on my skin stood up at the reverie. Unintentionally sinking into the memory, I closed my eyes and bit my bottom lip.

"Erica," my COO called my name. I'd blacked out in the middle of a colleague's presentation.

"What do you think of the new supply-chain proposal?"

I had no fucking clue what he was talking about, but I didn't miss a beat. "I think it has potential, but I'd like to spend more time with it this afternoon to take a deeper look. Is that okay?"

"Sure. It's fine, but I really need your input today."

"You'll get it. I promise."

Whew! It had been two weeks since my rendezvous with Zara, but I still felt her in the frequency of my womb. I still floated in the memories of our ascension to bliss. I think I'm going to live on the energy of what we shared for a while.

Zara was the most unlikely lover—a woman I'd only known and

mildly flirted with online in a group for erotic film and fiction fans. We'd gotten to know each other over seven months before the opportunity to take it offline presented itself. The chance came during a trip I took to Colorado Springs. I'd gone because I needed time away from the corporate rat race. I wanted separation from the day-to-day grind of productivity. And I needed a release from the pressures of everything. So, I booked a spur-of-the-moment trip to the mountain region. It was just the reprieve I'd needed.

I hadn't planned to meet Zara when I got there. I hadn't even remembered that she lived nearby when I booked my trip. Still, as I settled into my seat on the flight, I decided to check my messages one last time before going off the grid for a few days. That's when she came into the picture. Zara lived differently than me in many ways. She had long ago abandoned corporate America for a simpler life—a smaller home, a minimalistic and spiritual lifestyle. She was like a hippie who had benefitted from capitalism and then turned her back on the system in pursuit of more intentional living. When I told her about my plans to unplug for a few days in her hometown, she persuaded me to meet her for lunch before I left. As it turned out, Zara only lived 20 minutes from the Broadmoor Hotel, which would be my home away from home for the weekend.

"What do you say? I think it would be insane for us to be this close and not finally meet in person," she coaxed. "You can still have your alone time. Just save an hour or two for me. I'll even come to your bougie hotel to make it easy."

I giggled. "My days will be pretty full, but I can do a dinner."

"That's works, too."

"Cool. I'll text you once I touch down and settle in so we can make plans."

"I look forward to it," she'd responded.

Not long after our chat, the flight crew on my plane began their typical announcements. I tuned them out—too intrigued with thoughts of meeting Zara in person. She was a different kind of beautiful, unabashedly self-loving and boldly confident. Zara was open-hearted and had a glow from an inner-light that no make-up could match. Her voice had a timbre that could soothe a lonely heart with each word. I'd never told her how much I enjoyed chatting with her solely from a companionship perspective. With skin the color of sweet dark rum and a gaze that could pierce through one's armor, Zara's attractiveness had nothing to do with physical features. It had everything to do with her soul. I could feel her through our video chats but kept our interactions to playful banter about films, fiction, and culture. I was attracted to her, sure, but it felt innocent enough not to make a big deal about it. Besides, I never thought I'd meet her in person. That all changed when I arrived in Colorado Springs.

2

After three days of indulging in the bounty and beauty of nature by myself—from paddle boating on the water to yoga at sunrise and a horseback ride through the Garden of the Gods—I'd gotten what I needed out of my solo trip. I hadn't checked any work emails, ignored all phone calls, and I hadn't scrolled through social media. What I *did* do was enjoy exquisite meals alone. I ordered room service without a care about the cost or the number of calories in the food! I indulged and refused to feel guilty about it. This trip was for my soul. I gave in to the starvation of my spirit to enjoy life's pleasures with no condemnation attached. It was something Zara had encouraged during many of our conversations, but a struggle for me until that trip. It was also one of the first things we chatted about when she came to meet me at one of the hotel lounges—liberation.

I was excited to see her, and she didn't disappoint. Zara strode in, wearing an electric-blue off-the-shoulder dress with simple sandals. She had a huge afro that commanded the room. Her presence penetrated the space. Zara was like a queen arriving at her throne. The moment I saw her, my crush got heavy. Her mix of poise and counter-culture was a shock to the system, and I was hypnotized by it. She smiled broadly when she saw me.

"Erica! Hey, girl!" Zara outstretched her hands to pull me into a squeeze. Her hair smelled like passionfruit, and her skin felt like cashmere.

"Well, hello. It's wonderful to finally meet you. You look amazing!"

"Thank you," she paused to take me in. Zara nodded slowly, thoughtfully... affirmatively. "So do you." She revealed a gradual grin as if appreciating every second of the moment. "I'm glad you agreed to this."

"Me too. Want to grab a seat at the bar, a booth, or one of the main tables?"

"A booth would be nice. Those oversized chairs look cozy."

I was glad she chose the latter. I wanted the illusion of privacy.

UNFORTUNATELY, since we didn't have a reservation, we couldn't get the seating we wanted and ended up at one of the main tables. Thankfully, they were spaced out enough that we still had a little sense of aloneness.

Zara met me at the Penrose Room, a gorgeous restaurant inside the hotel I'd been staying in. It was early evening on my last night. Large windows allowed the dining room to be flooded with a twilight blue and purple sky. Lush mountains brushed the horizon outside while chandeliers shimmered above us like starlight. It didn't take much else to make the night feel like the beginning of a work of art. As the only two women of color in the restaurant, one of whom sported a crown of unapologetic black hair, we stood out like peacocks in a flock of hummingbirds. Even though Zara lived more of a hippie lifestyle, she still had an insane style to match the environment that night. We covered the typical small talk about my trip, and what I'd done so far, and why I just upped and ran away for a few days.

"What's been the best part of your getaway so far?" She quizzed between bites.

"Indulgence."

"Finally giving into your some of your cravings?"

"I am. And at least for a little while, dropping the weight of fulfilling everyone else's expectations. I slept. I ate. I played. I read trashy erotic stories, and I embraced solitude. Maybe acceptance is a better word."

"What do you mean?" She furrowed her brows in curiosity.

"I finally accepted that it is fine to want and have certain things without strings. I ate the cake, and I did *not* go to the gym afterward!"

Zara held back a cackle, but I could see the delight in her eyes. "Sounds perfect. That's freedom, and this is a great place for it," she said. "The region that is. I could live forever on the views and serenity here. It makes you want to just *be*, you know?"

"I think you could live anywhere based on how you've designed your life."

"True, but the eye-candy of nature makes pleasure that much sweeter. It's less to block out and more to drink in. Sort of orgasmic once you become at peace with being an ever-budding flower in it."

"Hm." Her word choice made me sit up a little straighter, but I didn't take the baton. "Interesting." I let the conversation simmer in a weighted pause.

Zara and I talked more about the online group where we met, some of the folks in it, and what drew us to each other outside of it. While we both obviously had a thing for eroticism in art, there was something under the surface that we hadn't discussed. Something kinetic. I felt a magnetizing pull and wasn't sure how much was equal on each side. So, I tried to ignore it and keep everything platonic. Too much was going on in my mind.

As we sat between courses, I realized everything could have been in my head. Zara was just being herself. I was the one fighting a life of boredom and overwork. The fact that she was so beautiful, graceful, and playful made it hard for me not to fantasize or project that there was more there than there was. At the time, I didn't know if she had an angle, but I enjoyed the ambiguity.

Zara entered my space like a comet striking Earth. She had a way of speaking and eye-gazing that made me dissolve into her world without putting up a fight. It was a joy-ride for a burnt-out corporate soul.

The time flew by quickly. Salads. Wine. Light fare. And finally, desserts. Dinner was ending quicker than I wanted it to. Thankfully, we had an attentive but seasoned waiter who didn't break up the flow. Our conversations were so refreshing and interesting. As time ticked on and more alcohol went down, I loosened my grip on trying to control the direction of the conversation. I wanted to savor it.

"I love your tattoo. I've been staring at it all night." I heard myself say to Zara. "What language is that, and what does it say?" She had an elegant script inked on her wrist.

"Thank you. It's Amharic. I'm Ethiopian, and it says, *A disciple of love.*"

"Wow. I love it."

"Thank you! It's a reminder of my purpose in life."

"What's that?"

"To study love; and to *be* love with my whole soul."

I melted. "You are so much." The words tumbled out of my mouth before I could stop them.

"Am I?"

"Yes. No! I mean, yes, but in a good way! A great way, actually." I fumbled but recovered as best I could. "I like your style. Your vibe. Your whole energy is aspirational is all I meant. Yes, that's it. I appreciate your energy."

"Thank you. Likewise. You're like a flower that wants to bloom, but is holding out for whatever reason. It's a shame we're winding down. I've enjoyed hanging out with you and could definitely talk longer."

"Is that right?"

"Very much! Next time, movie night! It's getting late though, and you have a flight tomorrow, so it's best we wind down."

"I like the sound of a next time."

"Me too."

After the waiter came and we cleared the tab, Zara and I politely ended our evening with a hug in front of the hotel property. It lasted longer than it should have and I think my open-mouth exhalation before releasing left a trail of warmth over Zara's earlobe. I didn't say anything though, hoping it didn't come off too forward. I hadn't planned it, but spending time with her put me so much at ease that the deep breaths came on their own accord.

"Have a safe flight back to Atlanta," she waved and smiled before turning to leave. She didn't address anything, but there's no way she didn't feel it.

"Thank you!" I rolled with it. "I'll let you know when I land."

MY BODY VIBRATED as I made my way back to my room. What the hell just happened? Was that a friendly dinner or a words-unspoken-first-date? Did she feel the same energy that I did or was I completely living in a fantasy? I didn't have the answers to my nearly twenty-one questions. What I did have thirty minutes later was a text from Zara:

"I REALLY ENJOYED meeting you tonight. I wish you weren't leaving tomorrow. 😶"

And just like that, my questions were answered. She'd felt what I felt and wanted more.

3

___

It was 11:48 PM when I sent the text. I wanted to extend my stay in Colorado if I could see Zara again. I thought about the five-word sentence for almost an hour before hitting send: "Are you free tomorrow night?" It was spontaneous but not impulsive, and I had nothing to lose. It took her twenty minutes to notice or respond. When she typed back "Yes," I felt a flutter in my chest.

"What's up?" She followed up with a short response of curiosity.

I told her I wanted to see her again, and when she asked about my return flight, I brushed it off. My nerves were a wreck, but I didn't stop myself. I wanted to go out on a limb. To act with a little courage. I took a deep breath and asked her if I could give her a call instead of texting. *God, I hope this isn't coming off creepy or too forward. It's creepy, but it's too late. Shit. What the hell were you thinking?* A tornado of thoughts upended everything in my head. I had to keep going. It would be even weirder if I'd dropped the conversation at that point. Thankfully, she agreed to a call. *How gracious.* My inner-thoughts were a mix of bravery, fear, and taunting.

"Hey, Erica," She answered through a smile. I could hear it. That was a good sign.

"Hey...sorry, I know it's late."

"No worries. So, what's going on tomorrow night?"

"Well, I had a really nice time with you this evening. And I was just thinking—and I hope this doesn't sound crazy—that I'd like to see you again." I took a gigantic breath. "Like, for a date? I mean, I don't know if you're interested. I won't be offended if you're not. I hope you don't think I'm nuts. I promise I'm not." I couldn't shut up! "Oh my god. This isn't going how I hoped!"

Zara let out a deep laugh.

Oooh shit, is all I could think. *I'm a joke. She's laughing at me. This was a dumb ass idea.*

"I don't mean to laugh," she apologized as if reading my mortified mind. "I had a great time too. I like you, Erica, and I really like what you just did there. I know that wasn't easy." Zara giggled again. "It was sort of adorable."

"Not in a Joe-Goldberg-*You* kind of way, was it?" I self-consciously referenced a hit Netflix show with a stalker for a lead character.

She cackled. "No! I'm choosing not to take it that way. Besides, I was hoping to hear from you sooner rather than later."

Yes! I made her laugh. "Whew!" Finally, I relaxed. "Well, that's a relief." I took a moment to gather myself. "So..."

"About tomorrow evening," Zara started finishing my sentence. "I'd love to see you if it's a possibility. I'm actually flexible for most of the day."

"Then I'll reschedule my flight. I just feel like this is an opportunity I don't want to miss. There's nothing significant for me to rush back to."

"I understand. There's a new erotic art museum not too far away that I think you'd enjoy. We could start there or maybe try something different like creating our own art. I have supplies. It's up to you."

"I like both ideas. This is exciting!"

"I bet you're glad you took the chance to call tonight."

"I am. I haven't done anything arts-related in a while. Not actively, I mean."

"We'll make tomorrow fun! No doubt about it. Why don't you give me a call in the morning? I'll get the logistics together for you so we can meet up. How does that sound?"

"Thrilling," I confessed. Zara was giving me everything I needed on what would have otherwise been a fitful evening of wondering what if. "I'm looking forward to it." I grinned. I felt accomplished. "I'll talk to you then."

"Good night," her voice fell to almost a whisper. Like a gentle kiss.

"Good night."

THE NEXT MORNING I woke up with teenage excitement but adult desires. I'd pushed my return flight out a day and extended my stay at the hotel for another night. I'd never done anything like I did the evening before and wasn't sure if I'd ever felt a rush of excitement and nervousness so strongly. My life was usually so structured that acting extemporaneously threw me for a loop, but I liked it. I loved that Zara drew it out of me. I wasn't sure what it was about her, but there was something that I couldn't resist. She was magic.

We spent most of the day together, starting with brunch and a stroll through a botanical garden before visiting the erotic art museum she'd mentioned. I'd never been to one and it was a fascinating collection of eroticism. The pieces varied from small and subtle to expansive and bold, but they were presented tastefully. Out of all the exhibits, the bondage section held my attention the most. Admittedly, it isn't a realm I'd explored much.

"Some of the photographs are intense, aren't they?" Zara struck up a conversation as we ambled down a hallway with large black and white prints of women in bondage. The models were of various ethnicities.

"Yeah. I don't know much about rope work. It's kind of beautiful."

"Hm," she quietly acknowledged my observation but didn't add much. She left me to absorb the art.

"Have you ever...uh..." I decided mid-question that it was a bad idea to ask what I was thinking.

"What?" It was too late. Zara had heard enough to want to know.

"Nothing. It's too personal to ask."

"I can make that decision for myself," she spoke dominantly, but her voice had a hint of charm—the sureness of it made me stand up straighter.

"I was just wondering...if you um...you know, had experience with restraints and bondage on this level." I was so embarrassed, but I felt like I owed her the rest of my question since I'd piqued her interest.

She smiled. "No. Not on this level. I have enjoyed some moments with a little restraint, but not with ropes. Mine were more gentle, using scarves or neckties," Zara added. "You seem interested."

"I'm curious."

She was silent again. I hated it because I desperately wanted to know what else was on her mind, but she didn't give another inch.

I LEARNED over the course of our day that Zara was a slow reveal in every aspect. She was thoughtful. Intentional. Alluring and enigmatic. I found myself following her lead, not just because it was her city and she was playing impromptu tour guide, but because I was falling under her spell whether she was actively casting one or not.

The day unfolded like a dream I didn't want to wake from. At some point, before leaving the museum, I heard myself confessing that I'd love to learn more about some of the art and would probably do a little digging online to learn more about rope bondage. That's when things shifted. We were grabbing a snack at a tapas bar and Zara placed her hand gently on top of mine. I trembled, but didn't pull back.

She leaned over to whisper, "Do you want me to teach you what I know?"

Our eyes locked and my lips parted slowly like flowers opening at dawn to taste the sun. "Yes..."

4

I returned to my hotel room, and Zara made a detour to her house to look for items she'd need to help me explore. I knew things were moving fast, but I didn't feel like I had anything to worry about regarding safety. Sure, we'd just met the day before but we had been talking for almost a year. If something was off, I would have felt it in my spirit. To the contrary, it felt as though she couldn't get back to me fast enough.

When Zara arrived at my hotel room, she was dressed in all black. Slender, with subtle sexy appeal, her clothes fit like a second skin. But Zara's big hair, big earrings and big bronze bracelets made her a beautiful paradox. She had a messenger bag slung over her shoulder, which I assumed contained whatever she'd gone home to get. Because I didn't know what to expect and I only had the clothes I'd traveled with, I was in a bathrobe with a matching mauve bra and panty set.

"Hey," I greeted her. "Come on in."

"Thank you. You look like you just left the spa," she teased.

"Well, I feel pretty rela—."

"Have a seat on the sofa," Zara gave me specific instructions and placed her bag down. She stepped out of her shoes and joined me on the hotel lounger. "We should go over a few things before we start." Zara brushed her hand against my cheek and peered at me with a friendly smile. "Erica," she started again. "You seem like an amazing person, and I enjoyed my day with you. Last night's dinner, too. I want to make sure that you're sure though." Zara stopped and let her hand drop to my leg. She drew an invisible line with her finger. "Are you sure you want to cross the line with me tonight—from friendship to lover?" She watched my face patiently.

Lover. The word's weight was nominal, but it still fell over me like chiffon over bare shoulders. I felt a chill thinking about her question, but the answer was easy. Nothing in me needed to give a second thought to sleeping with Zara. "Yes," I confirmed. "I'm sure."

She moaned in delight of my answer. "You are so attractive, Erica" Zara complimented. "I'm going to make sure you enjoy every second of this."

I clutched her hand and held my breath.

"The first rule is to breathe," Zara didn't miss a beat. "Your breath is going to play a big role in your pleasure, so relax," she caressed my jawline and ran her thumb over my lips. "The second rule is to trust me. I'm going to introduce you to a few new things that I think you'll enjoy, but if there's anything that you don't like just say so."

I smirked. "Should I have safe word?" Suddenly, I became nervous.

"You won't need one, I promise," she looked me directly in my eyes. "And...rule number three, lose yourself. Let go! Let lust. Let passion. Let *feelings* rain down on you. Let desire out and have fun!" Zara tapped my leg playfully and reached for her messenger bag.

I was a see-saw of ease and angst. She slowly slid my bathrobe off to reveal my bra and panty set. Zara kissed my shoulder slowly and moved down my arm with a trail of kisses. When she neared my forearm, she raised it to reach her lips and continued her journey of pecks down to my hand and fingertips. She held my gaze as she brushed the top of my hand with her lip. Her eyes glinted from a smile within.

"Remember to breathe," she whispered.

The next thing I saw was her pulling a blindfold out of her bag and placing it over my eyes. It was warm and smelled like jasmine. She turned on music and guided me to sit on a different chair—the one at the desk. Zara then lowered herself in front of me—I could feel the warmth of her breath pass over my knees—to tie my legs to the feet of the chair. She used a soft fabric. The knot was secure, but not so tight I couldn't break free if I really wanted to. She kissed me. Up my calves, on my quads, in my thighs, all while using her hands to caress my sides and stomach. Zara cuffed my hands behind my back with something strong, leather maybe.

I whimpered. A little in nervousness, but mostly in arousal. I couldn't believe I'd wanted this, and I was surprised that she agreed. I was also shocked that I sank into it with so few reservations. Zara walked away and returned with something that gently tickled me. It was light, and made blood rush to the surface of my skin. *A feather,* I'd guessed. My body relaxed, and from head to toe, I felt tingles.

Zara moved around me fluidly, and the music became more pulsating and entrancing. After rousing me with the feather, I felt the full extent of her palms rubbing my shoulders. I could feel her behind me. She warmed up my shoulders up with her touch before immediately introducing another toy. *Slap!* I felt the sting of leather tassels hitting my skin. Zara moved with rhythm, in flow with the music. She followed harder lashes with soft rubs until I felt myself swaying. This went on for a while, and I enjoyed every second of it. Zara eventually untied me and helped me to my feet.

"Easy. Take your time standing up," she coached. "Watch your step."

I felt as though I was rising from the edge of a subspace. A little more sensory play might have thrust me into an even higher state of awareness. I was excited. I wanted more.

Zara guided me to the bed. "Lay down on your stomach," she instructed.

I complied, reassured to have my hands and feet unbound but still curious of what was next. She took a few moments to come back and I could hear her placing things on the nightstand. Soon after, I felt the weight of Zara on the bed and her hands unclasping my bra. I felt her skin. *She took off her clothes...oh my God.* My body shuddered on contact with hers. I was still wearing the blindfold and still couldn't see, but I could feel her climb on top of me—how warm she was. The next thing I sensed was Zara rubbing her hands together before she placed them on me for long, slow, oily massage strokes. She moved purposefully, paying attention to my whole body. Zara touched me with a dominant tenderness. She put her entire being into stroking me, touching and kissing wounds on my skin that even *I* didn't know were there. Wounds of loneliness. Wounds of resentment. Wounds of wanting but rarely getting. Wounds of exhaustion, and hunger. Wounds of life.

She soon paused to get a toy to stimulate my skin beyond her touch. It was prickly, and sharp. My body tensed instinctively. I didn't recognize it, but I trusted her. Zara moved at an unhurried pace, silently assuring me that I was okay. I felt the tool scraping the length of my back and the curves of my ass. It felt like the tip of an icepick with enough pressure to awaken but not harm my skin. Eventually, she put down whatever she was using and followed up with something cold. Something thin and steel against my spine. I had no idea what it was. Zara let it rest there while she kneaded the small of my back and the roundness of my ass. I felt myself getting slicker and dampening the sheets beneath me.

As I lay in complete surrender to her touch, Zara removed the cold steel and dragged her nails against my back. The next thing I felt was a series of hot drips on my back quickly followed the cool wind from her breath. *What is that?* It took me a few moments to guess that it was probably candle wax. I writhed and bucked, folded and unfolded from the adventure of it all. The fire and ice took me over the top and I screamed in pleasure.

"Oh my god," I moaned. "Oh my God, oh my—"

"Goddess!" She corrected me and spanked me at time.

I think I came from the shock. The moment was electrifying and nothing short of orgasmic. "Zara," I cried in desire. I wanted to grab a hold of her.

She quietly helped me move to my left side to temper my excitement and pace the pleasure. Zara held me from behind and brought a hand to my mouth. She cupped my face with one hand while her other arm encircled me. I couldn't see or speak then. She gagged me with her palm, and her free hand danced around my stomach. She rubbed and scratched and grabbed me while muzzling my screams. Zara alternated using her hand, forearm and even a single finger to trace the contours of my body.

I was drunk from the experience by then. Between the music and the sensory play, I was overwhelmed and drenched with desire. Zara took me on experience beyond the boundaries of my body. The way she rotated between tenderness and toughness was so foreign to me. It was thrilling.

Zara flipped me onto my back and brought back the flogger. It felt like she might have two this time. She whipped my stomach, my breasts, and my thighs with precision, and followed-up with soft touches of her hands. She brought me up and back down, and back up again. She straddled me, and I could feel her hot wetness oozing on to me. Zara leaned down to come nose to nose, breasts to breasts with me. And finally, she kissed me. I lost it. Her lips tasted like guava and I couldn't get enough.

My legs shook and my arms vibrated, but Zara took her time with me.

"Remember to breathe," she reminded me. "Breathe from your pleasure center, bring those breaths up your stomach, to the top of your head and down your spine back to your root. Circulate the energy," she instructed me.

I could feel her watching me. She pulled my panties off and rubbed my inner thighs. She moved up to my face again, caressing my chin again. My eyebrows. My cheekbones.

"Open your mouth a little," she whispered.

I did, and she traced my lips with a piece of fruit. *Strawberry*. I stuck my tongue out to play with it. I French kissed it the way I wanted to kiss her. Zara purred in response. I squirmed. It was almost too much.

"Bite it," she commanded. "Eat it." Zara smacked my skin.

I devoured it. "Mmm."

When she finally slid the blindfold off, I melted. She was strikingly beautiful. Attentive and powerful, I had *never* slept with anyone like her. I'd never been with anyone who had paid attention to all the creases, corners and curves of my body and mind. Zara brought me to the edge. By noticing the forgotten places on my skin, Zara drew attention to areas of my body that even I hadn't paid attention to. She explored the spaces between each finger and toe, the inner creases of my elbows, the top of my ears just as much as my earlobes, my knees. Zara was masterful. She made pleasurable spots out of the mundane. Each contact from her got me high.

"I love your complexion and how you taste," I confessed.

"How's that?" she asked.

"Intoxicatingly sweet, with a little bit of fire. Like sweet dark rum."

"Well, I don't know if anyone has ever told you, but you glisten so beautifully when you're aroused. It's magical watching your pussy swell, expand and open up for me," Zara lowered her gaze to my yoni. "It's gorgeous." She studied me while running the tip of her finger against my inner lips, pressing in and squeezing them together. She massaged them. Zara caressed the edge of my labia and tugged at the tiny patch of hair I let adorn my mound. She reveled in me, and I sank into bliss.

Without another word, Zara gripped my hips and transported me to a hedonistic paradise with her tongue and fingers. We rolled all over the bed, indulging in each other's sticky-sweet nectar. Licking, lapping, sucking, kissing, and burying our faces into one another. The sex was playful but mindful. It was unburdened by expectations. The tone set by Zara allowed for all kinds of creativity and freedom. I felt safe with her.

"You feel soooo good," she moaned in my ear. "So. Fucking. Good!" Zara bit my earlobe before repositioning herself so she could look me in the eyes.

We held hands, upping the intensity through interlocked fingers as we grinded on each other. The orgasms flowed. They rushed out of me. Zara's energy knocked down the doors to my sensual existence. She broke the dam and expanded me into a freefall of sexual liberation. I didn't want the night to end.

With her fingers on my throat and her slippery beauty gliding against mine, Zara shattered everything I thought I knew about the possibilities of pleasure—about the power of spontaneity and trust. After hours of lovemaking, we finally cooled down. Exhausted. I kissed her shoulders and thanked her for the experience. It felt awkward to say it out loud, but my heart was so full of gratitude, and I couldn't help myself.

"Thank you for trusting me with your body. I wanted to honor it, and I hope you felt that," Zara said.

Her word choice was incredible. I needed to sit with it for a while. I kissed her again in return. No other words needed to be spoken.

5

The next morning as I prepared to check out, I reminisced on the day before. It was absolutely perfect, and I would never the same. When I'd made plans to visit Colorado Springs for a mental health break, there was no way I could have predicted the experience. Zara penetrated my being like a vibrant column of light. She was such an unexpected escape—a whole journey unto herself. She uplifted me.

Zara came into my world with ease but shook it to its core. Before meeting her, I was bored and overworked. My love life was non-existent. When I did have sex, it was underwhelming and often with people I knew weren't what I needed, but were enough to chase loneliness away. Work was my life, and I was near dead inside. Now, after just a few days of self-care and mind-blowing intimacy, I feel energized to be more intentional. I'd met so many new people over the last few years and not a single one, besides Zara, had such a profound effect on me in such a short amount of time. It was beyond sex. It was past orgasms. It was an awakening.

She stayed with me until late in the night. Neither of us wanted the evening to end, but she had to get back to her life and I had to prepare for my flight.

"I'd love to host you in Atlanta if you ever come for a visit, but if you don't..." I'd started extending an invitation.

"I like the sound of that." She smiled broadly. "Until then though, make sure you let me know you get home safely."

"I will."

"I'll be dreaming of you tonight."

"And I'll be reliving you all year!"

Zara chuckled. She gathered up all of things and put them in her messenger bag. She kissed me once more and pulled me into a deep embrace before leaving my hotel room. "Good night," she said.

"Good night. Thanks again for everything. This was one of the best weekends of my life. Truly." I didn't hold back on the honesty.

Zara gave me courage. I didn't even recognize myself. It was me who had requested everything. Even though she accepted and ultimately drove the experience, none of it would have happened if I didn't take the chance to ask for what I'd wanted. I'd been so sucked into her energy that a fearlessness surfaced that was new to me. I liked it. I loved the effect she had on me. Not only did I get what I wanted, I had no idea how out-of-this-world incredible it could possibly be. I was energized! I wanted to learn more. The way Zara touched me was like a torch lighting the path to ultimate orgasms and states of pleasure.

As I made my way out of the hotel and back on my flight, I replayed aspects of my entire weekend back in my mind. It was flawless. When I got back home, I vowed to make several changes in my life. From revamping my relationship with my job to creating more time to explore what I loved, what I experienced and what I wanted. I set an intention to learn more about the kind of lovemaking Zara exposed me to. I know that was the lightest form of dark sex—the whips, cuffs, and blindfolds, and all—but I wanted to know more about the way she controlled our energies. I was enthralled with the consciousness of it all. If there's one thing the whole experience taught me, it's that I'd gone my entire adult life barely scratching the surface of my pleasure potential. But I'd had a taste, I'd drank the elixir of her sweet dark rum and would never be the same. I wanted to live an intoxicated life.

END

CORSETS AND COGNAC

CHAPTER 1

Ashley's nerves lurched when she glanced at the calendar. Tech week. After three months of grueling rehearsals, her debut as a burlesque dancer loomed just four days away. The thought of performing in front of a live audience made her stomach swirl. From what she'd gleaned, the week ahead would be more demanding than the previous months as the cast and crew sought to tighten up the show. Ashley couldn't believe she'd let Kerry-Ann talk her into moving from student to performance partner—from learning the art of striptease for fun to taking off her clothes in front of a hundred strangers.

Ashley breathed deeply into her diaphragm and sipped a kale smoothie—her second breakfast. Since deciding to accept Kerry-Ann's challenge, Ashley's mornings started at 6:00 and were packed with intense stretching and two-hour workouts. She needed the energy boost. More than prepping her body, the fitness routine cleared Ashley's mind and helped maintain her resolve. Stepping on that stage would be a momentous move.

Just a few years ago, she inhabited a different world—one that was structured and predictable. Married and living in the suburbs of

Atlanta with a teenage son and two dogs, she'd coasted on a traditional trajectory. Becoming a retro vaudeville dancer? Not in her timeline. But then again, neither was witnessing her carefully-planned life shatter to pieces.

As Ashley moved from a formulaic existence to one of passion, she revisited hobbies she had once loved but abandoned decades ago —dance, piano, and hiking—and rededicated herself to them, intensifying her interest. She sought adventures.

Despite her performance anxiety, Ashley was proud that she'd committed to stepping into the spotlight. The butterflies were equally from fear and excitement about baring it all on stage. Dancing with Kerry-Ann and the rest of the cast would be liberating if Ashley could get through it, and she desperately wanted that win. For much of her life, she was a shy, soft-spoken follower who purposely avoided standing out in crowds.

A military brat who had grown up all over Asia, Ashley was half African-American and half Japanese. Her mother had joined the armed forces to escape poverty in the States and get a free education while traveling the world. She ended up falling in love with a lanky Japanese electrician while stationed at Kadena Air Force base in Okinawa and settled in Japan after completing her tour of duty.

Well-traveled, Ashley had visited ten countries before age twelve. When they moved their small family to the States, they settled in Key West, Florida. Like most kids uprooted in those hormone-laden years, Ashley struggled to fit in. She was chubby, had a different look, and a funny accent—she was constantly bullied for being different, making her teenage years almost unbearable. Ashley couldn't wait to leave when she graduated high school. She craved a more "black experience"—one that she'd seen depicted on TV shows like "A Different World"—to help her navigate her new home country in brown skin. She targeted the list of historically black colleges and universities and chose Spelman College.

There, Ashley fell in love with Atlanta. The diversity of people, the culture—music, dance, and the arts—sorority life and the giant difference between the city and the small beach town she'd called home, which was mostly occupied by tourists and retirees. Sure, she missed the ocean, but not as much as she loved her new location—enough to launch her career as a sushi chef, marry, and start a family. Ashley treasured that life for nearly two decades before making a careless decision that would entangle her in anguish for years to follow. Since the divorce, she had worked to design a new life and managed to fill every hole except for one—love. And she craved that deeply.

Ashley joined groups for single solo travelers, read books on becoming more desirable, dove into therapy sessions to heal from trauma, and learned to love herself as she rebuilt her self-confidence. Her days were full with running her catering business, dance rehearsals, and hobbies, but her evenings were empty. One of the benefits of having so many diversions—and apparently a new night job as an erotic dancer!—was that exhaustion sent her to bed early. Still, Ashley was ready to experience excitement with someone new. She wanted to travel and explore the world with a partner. It was time.

KERRY-ANN SAT on her enclosed deck enjoying a full plate of dumplings, and ackee and salt fish with chilled sorrel tea—a typical Jamaican breakfast. She was excited! In just a few days, she'd launch her brainchild *Corsets and Cognac*. Not only was she the choreographer for the new burlesque show, she owned its brand-new venue—The Crown. A decade-long dream come true.

While Kerry-Ann battled typical new-venture nerves, she mostly floated, invigorated and charged up. She'd triumphed over every friend, family member, and banker who had told her she couldn't do it. Everything wasn't perfect, but the night club looked damned good. Kerry-Ann had spent the last few months dealing with construction delays, contractor issues, and working with the attorneys to ensure all of her paperwork was in order. The work was draining but so satisfying. On this gorgeous spring day in Atlanta, she felt fearless.

Corsets and Cognac was a performance drenched in sensuality. Kerry-Ann had spent dozens of hours perfecting the show, wanting it to drip with intrigue and tease with seduction. Though she'd never lived in Jamaica, she leaned on her lineage for inspiration when creating dazzling costumes and selecting ideal diverse performers— women and men heavily representing the Afro-Latin diaspora, all incorporating their cultural beauties into a traditionally European presentation. Kerry-Ann's goal was a world fusion of arousing fantasy on stage. The cognac part of the equation would come from drink specials that highlighted brandy makers from all over the world. She hoped the unexpected and complex spirits would tease attendee palates and add a balance of masculinity to the evenings.

Kerry-Ann thrived on straddling the line between masculinity and femininity. She loved blending gender expression and embraced the harmonious union of the two. As she was down to the last bites of her breakfast, her phone rang. She picked up immediately.

"Hey, Daddy!"

"Morning, darling." Her father, Errol, was pleased to hear the joy in her voice. "How is everything going up there? You ready for your big night?" Errol quizzed, a hint of Jamaican accent slipping through. He still lived in Miami, where Kerry-Ann was born and raised.

"Almost," she answered before taking another sip of sorrel. "Things are hectic, but they're coming together nicely. I'm heading to the venue soon."

"Good. Good. You know..." Errol idled. "I am proud of all the work that you have done," he admitted. "I know I wasn't a big supporter, or even understander, of your dreams in the past, but I am happy to see you doing this. Something you love so much. I think your mother would have been pleased as well."

Kerry-Ann breath halted, her father's words falling over her like warm water washing away the final ashes of unease that once anchored them in tension. Her father was indeed not initially supportive of her dreams of becoming a dancer. He'd made it clear decades before when she inched toward high school graduation.

"Thank you so much, Daddy." Things had changed a lot since then.

"You come a long way from all of those little talent shows, ah?"

"Yeah!" Kerry-Ann beamed.

They shared a chuckle. At an early age, Kerry-Ann had developed a fondness for the arts and loved to perform as a child. From dance-hall reggae to Miami bass music, she grew up immersed in songs and became a self-taught choreographer. She'd competed in every youth talent show she could find in the late 90s, learning most of what she knew from hours in front of the TV watching music videos on BET and MTV. Kerry-Ann knew even then that her passion was rhythmic movement. Her parents, however, declared that there was no future in dancing, and though they could afford to, they would not finance her dream of preparing for a career in the arts.

"Bopping is for fun, Kerry-Ann, but it will not support a family," Errol had said at the time. "And mi nah pay fi pay fi dem sinting," he'd added in Jamaican patios. Devastated, with no money to chase her dream, Kerry-Ann instead studied film and television production at Miami-Dade Community College. Her passion for dance fizzled to something she did only at clubs with friends. To hear her dad's supportive words now overwhelmed her. The two *had* come a long way.

"Well," Errol said. "I only called to see if you needed anything else. I know you have a lot to do, so I won't hold you too long."

"I'm fine, Daddy. You've done so much already. Thank you!"

"All right, darling. I will call you later."

Kerry-Ann hung up and tears welled. Without her father's financial help, The Crown wouldn't exist. It was not by chance that he'd had a change of heart about supporting his daughter's ambitions. It was by way of tragedy. When Kerry-Ann was 28 years old, her mother died suddenly, rocking their small family and pushing Kerry-Ann and her dad into a nurturing embrace. Though it took several years for them to heal, individually and as a family unit, Kerry-Ann was grateful for the progress and loved him dearly. Now, on the precipice of launching her biggest dream, she was ecstatic to have Errol along for the journey. She wanted her club to be a game-changer, something unlike anything that existed in Atlanta. And she was confident she'd see her vision transform into reality.

CHAPTER 2

Tech week was indeed hell for both women. Full dress rehearsals with lights, sounds, props, and special effects—the cast and crew's final chance to test their production and make last-minute changes. Ashley repeatedly reviewed her role in the show, thinking through the provocative character she invented to play. She reflected on the fantasy she wanted to convey, and the duet she would act out with Kerry-Ann in a giant cage above the audience.

Wondering how she would lose herself in sensual abandon in front of so many onlookers, Ashley realized she'd never even done anything like that for her husband when she was married. She'd never fully *let go* in front of anyone. Never moved out of raw energy without worrying about how she looked. The only time she'd ever been on stage dated back to her days at Spelman when she pledged Delta Sigma Theta and had to take part in a performance. That was almost, 30 years ago in the late 90s, and there was nothing erotic about it.

Now, she was equally excited and terrified of taking on the role of a nymph-like exhibitionist. When Ashley danced in her current classes, the stakes were low. She was with a dozen other women who cavorted strictly as a hobby or for fitness. Maybe one other student had performance aspirations. Ashley didn't feel self-conscious about not having as athletic-looking a body as Kerry-Ann and some of the others, but she was nervous about being a part of an ensemble. A part of her knew the fear was ridiculous. Not only was she strong, flexible, and in-shape, she would be amongst a variety of body types in the troupe—a few ripped guys, others who were more slender, Kerry-Ann and her willowy physique, but also several like her, more of an average shape, but with incredible stamina.

Ashley's anxiety was around not looking like what she *thought* the audience would expect—a lithe dancer with a flat stomach. She was closer to a size eight than a size two with a size D bust. Her mixed heritage always made her exotic to others, which she admitted would likely play in her favor. With shiny tresses of blackberry-hued hair and skin the color of toasted sesame-seeds, Ashley was also delectably curvy.

"Everything is going to go smoothly," she comforted herself. "You know the moves. You've done them over a hundred times."

She tried giving herself a pep talk, but it ended up feeling more like ping-pong with two versions of herself: the confident and the insecure. For every affirmative statement she spoke aloud, a little nuisance voice inside of her countered. *Kerry-Ann is fit. She's danced her entire life. She's strong, with solid legs and chiseled arms. She's graceful. You? You're still trying to fit in, just a chubby blackanese girl.* Ashley recalled a term kids used to jeer at her when she lived in Key West.

Insecurities she'd thought were long gone bubbled to the surface. *Corsets and Cognac* drew out all of Ashley's vulnerabilities. "Not today," she pushed back on herself. "I'm strong too, and I can do this! I will."

Recovered from her grueling workouts earlier that morning, Ashley started packing her costumes for the first dress rehearsal. Heels. Sparkling stockings. Snap-off high-waisted panties. Thongs for under the panties. She'd purchased many of the items specifically for the show. A few pieces, she'd gotten from her mentor, Kerry-Ann.

Ashley now had pasties, jewelry, furs, more jewelry, and a custom-made corset that shimmered with star-studded gemstones. Burlesque attire was all about layers. About tiering tantalizing pieces of clothing so that each removal heightened sensuality. Ironically though, burlesque wardrobe had to be practical in its construction. Ashley made sure all of her items were easy to pull, zip, or tear off for a quick change—a tip from Kerry-Ann.

After making sure she had all of her costumes, Ashley loaded her hair and make-up supplies. It would all stay at the club for the duration of the show. From coconut oil to body make-up, hair rollers to glitter, she had everything. Red lipstick and big fake eyelashes were also a must.

Headdresses and other costume pieces would already be at The Crown. The more Ashley organized, the more settled she felt. Performing would be exhilarating. The chance to feel unflinchingly sexy in front of an audience was a dormant desire that she was afraid to admit even to herself. It lurked in her daydreams, and now, she would bring that daydream to life as part of a burlesque show.

WHILE ASHLEY JOSTLED unwanted inner thoughts, Kerry-Ann juggled entrepreneurial and producer woes. Her days would be long this week. Fifteen hours, at least. Not only was Kerry-Ann rehearsing the entire show, she was also making sure her bartenders mastered the cognac specials, receiving last-minute delivery items, approving and adjusting all the design elements and tweaking front-of-house—the audience seating area, holding and foyer space. Once she'd taken ownership, Kerry-Ann had transformed the 2500 square foot space from a grungy dive spot to an intimate sanctuary.

The Crown sat on the edge of the Virginia Highland neighborhood in Atlanta. Flanked by eclectic bars and restaurants, its location pulsed with foot traffic from residents just as diverse as its commercial neighbors. In Kerry-Ann's mind, there was no typical customer for burlesque shows. Men and women of various socio-economic backgrounds enjoyed the performances, as did those who identified as either straight or LGBTQA+. The key to drawing the best patrons lay in her marketing of the show as a scintillating experience with a middle-of-the-road price point—more than the college-aged demographic would want to part with but not too much to discourage working-class adults and beyond. More than anything, Kerry-Ann wanted audiences who would appreciate the experience and spread the word to ensure high-demand for future productions.

The Crown was over the top with visual splendor. A wall of mirrors with ornate gold frames and a giant chandelier cast a diamond-in-the-sun sparkle over the foyer. Merlot-hued drapes separated the lobby from the performance space, and whimsical touches accented corners, like a carnival horse on a pole. Even the restrooms were dramatic. Semi-transparent waterfall walls punctuated by colored LED lights lit up the sink areas. Posters of lingerie-clad models adorned the stall walls.

Still, with all the work Kerry-Ann had put into the space and production, there were issues.

"What do you mean the cage rig isn't secure?" she questioned her lead technical staffer, Todd.

"It's not safe for any performers to go in there as it is. Not enough air space for it to swing the way you want. We gotta do something about it sooner rather than later!"

"Okay, okay. So, where should we move it? We only have so much space." Kerry-Ann didn't linger on problems for long. She was all about solutions.

"I think we need to put it more in a corner than center stage. We should also shift other elements of the set to swing more diagonally."

"Won't that mess up the lighting design?"

"Yes," Todd spoke matter-of-factly. "Sorry."

Kerry-Ann resisted becoming flustered. She grabbed the back of her neck, giving it a good squeeze to stop tension from building. *Breathe it out*, she reminded herself, her strategy for smothering embers of stress. Redoing the lighting design would take time and money. Neither of which she had to spare. "All right. Let me think a minute." Kerry-Ann rubbed her hands together and then over her face.

"We could use a different apparatus," Todd suggested.

"No." She didn't waste a second pushing back. "That's a crucial part of the show. It's not optional. I want everything as we planned it. Just reposition the cage and I'll make sure everything else is updated to match."

"Copy that." Todd was energized by his boss's decisiveness. He'd been on the circus side of performance arts for almost nine years and had seen what happened when a leader was cavalier about safety or too stubborn to rework tech issues in the final hour.

With Kerry-Ann in charge, there was order, even during moments of high stress. *Corsets and Cognac* was her baby and she wanted everything to be as safe as it was beautiful. A dozen people were a part of the performance—an aerial silks artist, pole dancer, four street dancers, a four-piece R&B band, and two burlesque showgirls—Ashley and herself. Kerry-Ann was also comfortable with silks. Plus, at least another half a dozen people working behind the scenes ensuring the show was fluid and seamless. Kerry-Ann put her all into making sure the plans she'd dreamed up and executed would yield the results she desired. *Everything is going to be fantastic,* she told herself. *Have faith. You were born for this.*

BY THE TIME Ashley arrived at The Crown, she had found it unexpectedly quiet. The band hadn't set up and there were a few tech folks laser-focused on their tasks. Todd buzzed about with the energy of a skittish squirrel. Kerry-Ann was engrossed in a conversation on her phone but acknowledged Ashley with a smile and wave.

Ashley made her way to the dressing room to claim a corner and set up. Excitement surged from the energy of the performers in the back. Most had already arrived and taken their spots. Some did cognac and Bailey's Irish Cream shots while others were absorbed in taking selfies. Ashely quickly embraced the spirit, and a thrilling wind built in her chest. The spectacle of what she was about to embark on gripped her, seductive and transfixing.

"Helloooooo, everybody!" Kerry-Ann entered like lightning, sparking a new current of energy.

"I'm so excited about this week!" one of the street dancers exclaimed.

"Yup!" A wave of agreement emanated from everyone in the dressing room.

"Me too," Ashley added.

The room was a kaleidoscope of creativity revving up to create something beautiful.

"I'm glad to hear it." Kerry-Ann smiled at Ashley before speaking again. "If everybody could just stop what they're doing for a moment." She cleared her throat. "I want to talk to you before we go out for our first day of tech."

A hush fell and everyone's attention was on Kerry-Ann, who stood tall, letting the silence settle before speaking again. "I've already spoken to the folks in the band, and I want to talk to you, too," she began. "Everyone here has worked so hard over the last couple of months to create a magical performance, and now we're down to the final rehearsal days. Our last chance at perfecting it. I see all of the gorgeous costumes and know that our hard work will pay off more than we can imagine. *Corsets and Cognac* is going to be sexuality unleashed! Stimulating striptease and eye-popping showmanship. We're going make it sensual, seductive, sultry...and *glamorous*," Kerry-Ann continued her pep talk. "I don't know about you guys, but I'm ready to give audiences the time of their lives!"

Whoops and hollers burst out of the troupe.

Kerry-Ann took a moment to meet every performer's eyes individually before finishing. "Everybody looks great! I'm amped up at the sight of you!" She clasped her hands together and smiled. "When we go out there to rehearse, I want you to remember the end goal—and that's to embody your characters. I want you to give them 100% of your effort. Let's make it entertaining. Let's make it sexy! And most of all, let's make it fun! Are you guys ready?"

"Yes!" everyone responded in unison.

"I said, *are you ready*?" Kerry-Ann ratcheted up the intensity.

"Yes!"

"All right let's go put the final touches on this show. It's going to be incredible!"

CHAPTER 3

The first dress rehearsal was a train wreck. Kerry-Ann's Assistant Director botched all of the cues. Several performers got stuck in their costumes, messing up the timing of the show, and glitches riddled a few of the audience fly-over scenes. At the end of the first run-through, the 60-minute show clocked in at almost two hours. Kerry-Ann had to huddle with Todd and others in the crew to dissect every mishap so they wouldn't happen again.

Stress gripped Ashley. Anxiety replaced excitement among the cast. And the band was bored. It would take two more days before the production came together the way everyone had hoped. By then, they had rhythm. They had sex appeal. *Corsets and Cognac* had legs and was ready to take flight. With just forty-eight hours to go before opening night, the performance blossomed into something whimsically beautiful. Another thing was building too—something Ashley nor Kerry-Ann had expected. Sexual tension.

A loosely scripted show, *Corsets and Cognac* was a series of several independent acts tied together by a theme of sensual expressions of dance, acrobatics and gymnastics. Ashley and Kerry-Ann both performed with groups of shirtless men and each had racy solos.

During the final rehearsals, the two women sank deeper into their roles of vixens and their shared energy grew more tender and erotic. The slower musical choices were sultry melodies with heavy bass.

Ashley watched from the wings of the mainstage as Kerry-Ann rehearsed her solo in a gleaming corset that radiated the power of a sexual sentient. Kerry-Ann had drawn inspiration for its design from femme fatales that she'd studied over the years. Accented by feathers, gemstones and satin embroidery, Kerry-Ann's wardrobe fit tightly against her skin, casting spellbinding sparkles across the stage when the lights hit her. Her facial expressions pierced and entranced Ashley as she moved. It was as if Kerry-Ann was slowly masturbating on stage without touching herself. She embodied pleasure and passion radiated from Kerry-Ann's mood—her closed eyes, focused energy, furrowed brows and slightly parted lips, her intentionally seductive breaths. The fantasy Kerry-Ann conjured as she danced to the sultry blues music was like watching a thousand rose petals float on water. She was enchanting and her performance gave Ashley goosebumps. As much time as the two women had spent together, Ashley had never looked at Kerry-Ann the way she did that night. The way she imagined a patron in the front row would.

Kerry-Ann soon gyrated over to the wings opposite Ashley and stripped down to white lingerie. An elongated silk fabric dropped from the ceiling for her to ease into her next performance. Once she went backstage, she was joined by another scantily-clad aerial artist. Both of them scaled up the fabric and flipped upside down in unison. Watching them was dreamlike. Fog machines and strobe lights added to the alluring visuals of them upside down with their legs spread upward in perfect V-positions. The band segued to soul music next. In the back of the seating area, a camera was set up so that Kerry-Ann could later review the production from the audience's vantage point.

This show is definitely going to make people forget about their lives for a while, Ashley thought. When it was her turn to practice her solo, Ashley sashayed onto the stage after an introduction from the MC. Her slot was jazzy and up-tempo, more playful sexy than steeped in slow erotic movements. Ashley was frisky as she stepped out of her fur stole and white sheer dress to twirl, bop and shimmy around the stage. She caressed her face, ran her hands across her shoulders and chest. She became a wonder as graphics twinkled on the screen behind her to create the illusion of a perfect night sky, with her dancing in the dark ocean of heaven. Ashley's confidence deepened after more practice and chats with other performers, and Kerry-Ann's one-on-one pep talks. She felt carefree and gorgeous on stage by herself now, loving every minute of it! When it was time to rehearse the cage scene with Kerry-Ann, however, things felt a little tenser.

Both women had changed into sequined catsuits. The sparkly costumes allowed them to move more fluidly while visually dazzling the audience. Kerry-Ann had choreographed a salacious routine for them that called for getting close, caressing each other, climbing on top of each other like feral cats while undressing one another. It required trust and devotion to the passion of the moment. They would separate only to do slow, coordinated hip gyrations then twirl back into each other's arms. Ashley and Kerry-Ann were the final act, ending the show in a rotating filigree cage that ensured the entire audience would see them. As they rehearsed, Ashley felt a simmering voltage at the intensity of Kerry-Ann's stare an/d touch. Shockingly, she felt physically aroused for the first time. Ashley's breathing sped up and her heartbeat quickened.

"You're doing fantastic," Kerry-Ann whispered in Ashley's ear during a break.

"Thank you." Ashley was dizzy. Spinning in a cage is always fun and sexy until you stop. That's when the wooziness set in, a sensation Ashley found hard to get used to. Not to mention her body's unexpected pleasure response to Kerry-Ann.

"Come here. Sit down for a bit." Kerry-Ann slinked down to the edge of the stage and patted the space next to her. "I'm so proud of you. You've come a long way."

Almost everyone else had retreated to the dressing rooms. One performer lingered out front and noticed the build-up of energy between the women. Neither Ashley nor Kerry-Ann saw his presence in the darkness off-stage.

Ashley blushed. She hadn't anticipated such flattery. "I couldn't have done it without you. Thank you for believing in me and nudging me past my boundaries."

"You've always had sumptuousness inside. You just needed the right person to pull it out."

"I guess that person was you." The words slipped out of Ashley's mouth before she could think about them.

Kerry-Ann locked eyes with her. She half-grinned, trying to hold back the delight at Ashley's response. "Maybe."

Kerry-Ann had quietly had a crush on Ashley for some time now but did a great job hiding it. She didn't want to mess up their platonic friendship and didn't want to jeopardize the show. Kerry-Ann wasn't even sure if Ashely liked women. They'd only talked about their personal lives once, when Ashley mentioned having an ex-husband and a son, but didn't elaborate further. But this evening felt different. They'd both spent countless hours together and supported each other when they were running on fumes. Now, as they inched closer to opening night, each rehearsal felt more intimate than the last. Kerry-Ann had a hard time keeping her crush at bay.

"Yeah..." Ashley finally responded. "I guess I did have it in me."

"Of course you did." Kerry-Ann smiled. She cautiously placed her hand on Ashley's knee.

The contact of Kerry-Ann's fingertips to Ashley's legs sent Ashley's senses into a tailspin. It had been years since she felt that kind of energy from another woman. Even though they were close in the show, Ashley had sectioned that off in her mind as just art. Just fun. But now the way Kerry-Ann's fingertips fell onto her skin was like honey slowly seeping from a crystal goblet. The performance area was dark except for a few orange stage lights and time crawled to a stop. The voyeur in the back still went undetected. Although he couldn't hear them, he could see them. His brows furrowed.

Nerves shot through Kerry-Ann but she couldn't pull back her hand. Ashley's heartbeat instantly shot from a steady pace to a wild beat. She brought her gaze up to meet Kerry-Ann's and they shared a soundless moment. Ashley wanted to retreat, but she struggled. The touch had plunged her entire being into a world she'd worked hard to avoid. *Women.*

"Hell yeah, we did that shit!" A few of the dancers emerged from backstage and sliced through their moment like a machete.

Ashley and Kerry-Ann stood up swiftly. The onlooker slinked out of the shadows and joined the boisterous few who had just emerged. It was time for one more run through before calling it a night.

"All right, everybody. Let's give it all we've got!" Kerry-Ann seamlessly jumped back into work mode.

Ashley's shock from what they shared vanished just as quickly.

Seeds of curiosity from their castmate had been planted. He wondered, *what was up with those two?*

CHAPTER 4

Opening night arrived in a flash. The final dress rehearsal felt more like a dream, and suddenly, the full cast was all backstage preparing for their premiere. They could hear the murmur of the audience, awaiting the performance. While the dressing room whirred with adrenaline and excitement, up front, the lights were dim. House music played and the club was full of eager patrons sipping cognac concoctions of cinnamon and hibiscus. Kerry-Ann did an incredible job building demand for the show and Atlanta residents had shown up!

Several of the performers got flower deliveries to congratulate and wish them good luck. Ashley noted that she wasn't one of the recipients. She didn't have anyone in her personal life to back her on this journey, but she forged ahead anyway. Kerry-Ann was there for her as a mentor and an Ashley-didn't-know-what-now sort of way. Before they started the show, Kerry-Ann gave one more speech to the group to pump them up. Separately, she encouraged Ashley to give it her all.

"I know you're a little nervous. Trust me," Kerry-Ann comforted. "I am too. But you're an amazing performer. You can do this!" she added. "I'll be there with you the whole time." She squeezed Ashley's hand.

"I know. It's just...wow. So much more real now. There's a paying audience out there!"

"And you are a part of the magic they paid to see! Remember that. Remember your charm, and your inner goddess. Channel her. I want to see—no, I want to *feel* her tonight. You are so damned beautiful, Ashley. You got this!" Kerry-Ann winked.

Ashley nodded in agreement. She felt sexier just listening to Kerry-Ann.

"Whatever you do – give it 100% of your efforts, and everything will be fine," Kerry-Ann finished.

"Okay."

Just before Ashley got up to take her place, a text from one of her top catering clients pinged from her phone. *Ashley, I had no idea you were a dancer! My wife and I decided to check out this show and I just noticed YOU were on the flyer. Wow! Looking forward to seeing a different side of you! ;)*

"Holy fuck." The message sucked the wind out of Ashley. She gulped. Unsure how to respond, hoping her phone didn't send a read-receipt. Her confidence was rattled, but there was nothing she could do but go on with the show. "Oh well..." she mumbled to herself before putting her phone away. She would respond later.

THE SHOW WENT WELL, with cast members beginning to roam the theatre in feather and LED-lit costumes before the official start. A comedic emcee opened the evening with lots of laughs and moved the spectators through a night of Afro-influenced hedonistic artistry. From up-tempo routines punctuated by provocative dancers who channeled the zeal of West Indian carnivals to slow, uninhibited performances that oozed theatrical romance, the band helped steer the multi-cultural flow of sounds from steel drums of the islands to brassy jazz numbers reminiscent of New Orleans.

The props ranged from a sparkling foam cactus used to conjure phallic energy to a red-lipped shaped chair that playfully twisted the audience's imagination in a forbidden way. Felix, one of the lithesome male dancers, underscored the slow blues numbers by mesmerizing patrons with his strength and flexibility during a solo. He invited a female audience member on stage to take a seat in a chair he'd dragged on and slowly peeled off the layers of his costume until he was down to a mask, sparkling briefs and boots.

The guest on stage squealed. The crowd howled. Felix relished.

"Oooh yeaaaah, ladies and gentlemen!" The MC chimed in. "This gentleman has a lot more to show you so don't take your eyes off the stage!"

A pole that had been previously concealed from view was revealed and Felix crawled on all fours toward it before leaping into a gravity-defying routine of sheer male strength. His prowess on the pole set the tone for Ashley and Kerry-Ann's finale. As the show drew near its end, most costume pieces were abandoned and only the bare minimum covered the women.

Patrons were breathlessly engaged from beginning to end, more than a few participated in certain scenes when encouraged to volunteer by the MC. Hoots, hollers, cheers, and handclapping peppered the evening all night, especially when a fan went on stage and answered raunchy questions. The drink specials worked their magic, loosening everyone up to get swept into Kerry-Ann's alluring vision. A few cues were missed but no one in the audience could tell. The cast did a fantastic job of improvising when something unplanned happened.

Ashley's solo went better than she expected, and her scene with Kerry-Ann exploded into a scintillating masterpiece of athleticism. She wiggled. She pranced. She thrust her hips and let dozens of diamond-like props scatter from crevices of her costume. Kerry-Ann kept intense eye contact with Ashley throughout, whispering encouragement in her ear and teasing her with soft touches throughout their performance. Ashley had abandoned her fears, and all of the synergy they'd built up over the last few months splashed to the surface that night. Her curiosity about the intentions of Kerry-Ann's touches were ripe. So was her deep-seated desire to feel more of them.

Since their duet closed out the show, Ashley and Kerry-Ann had all eyes on them for every movement. They frolicked and floated, erotic exhibitionism on full display. Moving in unison and sometimes with synchronized breath, their performance created intimacy between them in a way neither anticipated. A few of their castmates noticed the uptick in passion between the women. Ashley felt seduced, Kerry-Ann's strong gaze and naughty beckoning hypnotizing her. The more Kerry-Ann sunk into the character of the ultimate seductress, the more she fell under her own spell. By the time the two ended their segment and grabbed hands for a bow, the electricity between them was formidable. Ashley trembled with craving. She'd forgotten about her client in the audience. Until he made eye contact with her. Ashley froze in fright and self-awareness, but he simply smiled and gave her an enthusiastic thumbs-up while mouthing great job! Whew. Her chest shook when she let out a sigh of relief.

"Thank you!" She waved at him and his wife enthusiastically. Their genuine response was permission to bask in the glow of conquering her fears and checking off a major milestone in the self-confidence department.

For all involved, the first show went by quickly—almost in a blur, an overwhelming success complete with a standing ovation. The crowd loved the mélange of mythical beauties journeying the stage in audacious costumes that melted away to G-strings and tasseled pasties.

"Thank you so much!" Kerry-Ann acknowledged the audience and invited the entire cast back on stage for a final bow.

Wrapping up opening night, Ashley felt exhilarated by a sense of pride and personal power. She felt accomplished and was also thrilled for Kerry-Ann. While performing was frightening, she could only imagine the stress of opening the club, managing it, and marketing it on top of creating the *Corsets and Cognac* brand.

"Congratulations!" Ashley exclaimed when she and Kerry-Ann were alone. The cast had all left after having a short, post-show celebration. "You did it!" Ashley instinctively pulled Kerry-Ann into a hug.

"Thank you!" Kerry-Ann sank into the embrace before slowly pulling away. "I feel like I can breathe easier now. Every night after this will be a breeze."

"It will. I had an amazing time out there," Ashley confessed.

"Good. I'm glad. You've worked so hard and looked so good, I'm happy to see you finally noticing and feeling it for yourself." Kerry-Ann flitted away just as soon as the words escaped her lips.

"Hey, where are you going?"

Kerry-Ann didn't answer but quickly returned. "These are for you," she said, presenting a bouquet of white lilies from her locker. "I didn't want to give it to you in front of everyone else because it might raise questions or have folks thinking I'm playing favorites, but I got these for you."

Ashley's heart skipped a beat. Uplifted by the gesture, she took a pleasurable sigh. She stared at Kerry-Ann in pleasant disbelief, and admired her cheekbones, her strong eyebrows and jawline. Ashley took in Kerry-Ann's soft shoulders and edgier parts, like her heavily pierced ears that were adorned with ruby studs all around them. Even her sassy, bob-styled wig. Kerry-Ann's bang hung just above her beautifully arched eyebrows.

"I don't know what to say," Ashley blushed as she took the flowers.

"You don't have to say anything."

A hush fell over both women. Energy whirled between them. Before they could speak again, however, some of the front-of-house staff came back to say that everything was ready to be locked up for the night.

"Thanks," Kerry-Ann acknowledged them.

Ashley, Kerry-Ann, and a few others exited at the same time for safety. As they approached their cars, parked side by side, Kerry-Ann seized their final moment to take a risk.

"Hey," she said as she hovered between her car door and the interior of her vehicle. "I um...I...I was wondering if you wanted to grab lunch tomorrow. We don't have to talk about the show."

Ashley gasped. Despite their chemistry, she wasn't expecting the request. She tapped the hood of her car nervously. A part of her wanted to accept immediately, but a bigger part screamed no. She felt thrust into a conundrum. How could she say no after Kerry-Ann had showered her with so many compliments and even bought her flowers when no one else did? *Easy*, her subconscious taunted her, *just say it politely*.

"I would love to," she began, "but...I have some existing plans already." Getting the words out were a challenge. She'd never lied to Kerry-Ann before. Ashley didn't have anything to do the next afternoon.

"Uh. Okay. Sure!" Kerry-Ann gulped. Rejection. It stung but she kept the conversation on track. "Well, I guess I'll see you tomorrow night then!" She forced a grin.

"See you," Ashley reciprocated the smile. She felt like an asshole.

Kerry-Ann skulked into her car and chastised herself for making a move. Not only could it throw off the energy of the show if Ashley was put off by Kerry-Ann's invitation, the move violated her personal rule of not dating students. Ashely was a former student, but still. Now she was also an employee—even worse! Kerry-Ann felt like an idiot.

Ashley slid into her driver's seat with ricocheting nerves. She'd had such a wonderful evening and now she was unsure if she was rude to the one person who had been rooting for her all along. What if Kerry-Ann just wanted lunch without an ulterior motive? What if she just wanted to meet up platonically? Ashley second-guessed her response all the way home. The truth was she that was not interested in dating a woman again—yes, she'd done it before—no matter how smart, beautiful or kind they were, she'd decided she didn't want to go there again. Ashley was lonely, but she wanted a boyfriend. She missed the feeling of big, strong hands pulling her into an embrace. She ached to smell the scent of an aquatic cologne waft by her on a date. *Just play it cool tomorrow*, she told herself.

CHAPTER 5

The next morning, Ashley chose to do her fitness routine outside instead of at the gym. She went to one of her favorite green spaces, a tranquil swath of wilderness just outside of Atlanta's City limits called Sweetwater Creek State Park. Several movies had been filmed there and remnants of an old steel mill that stood in the embrace of the rushing creek had become a focal point. Prior to giving her all to *Corsets and Cognac*, Ashley went to the park at least three times a week. Sometimes she'd hike the trails, other days she'd use the outdoor gym equipment, and other instances, she would park her convertible Jaguar in front of the waterfront and stare into the distance. On this day, she'd chosen a combination of all of those things.

It was 7:00 and quiet when she arrived. Ashely started with the shortest hiking trail before making her way to a cluster of outdoor gym equipment. Pull-ups, dips, hip flexors, core and glutes, she worked her upper body, but didn't push to muscle fatigue because she had to reserve energy for that night's performance. She did push hard enough to feel tingles of accomplishment for sticking to her goals and eating clean, however. Ashley then drove to the waterfront to cool down rather than walk to it—that would have been too long of a trek. When she arrived, she had the area to herself for nearly thirty minutes before an interracial couple pulled up in a black pick-up truck.

While Ashley reclined with the top down, she could sense the vitality of the duo who had just arrived. They were in love. Since she had chosen not to take up space on one of the park benches facing the creek, it was left open for them. Ashley stole glances at them from behind her shades as they made their way down to a picnic table. They were giddy, with little bags of food and drinks in tow. Ashley watched as the lovers sat down and the woman leaned onto the man's shoulder. He placed his arms around her, gently stroking her as a red cardinal zipped by. A sadness fell over Ashley; though she was witnessing love, with a backdrop of birds chirping and squirrels scampering about, she found herself longing for affection. She looked away.

Every now and then a fish would leap out of the water before quickly dipping back down—a reminder from nature that sometimes you have to get out of your comfort zone. Through her rear-view mirror, Ashley spotted deer milling around in the trees near a few cabins. A gust of wind blew over, ruffling the leaves and planting a cool kiss to her skin. Were it not through the lens of her loneliness, the scene around Ashley would be like a fairytale.

Neither the man or the woman was preoccupied with their phones, and every now and then he excitedly pointed as a bird or some other animal came into view. They were under an awning of trees, their own limbs entangled. He fed her carrots and grapes while she played in his scruffy blond beard. Ashley soon started her car and put the top back up. Their intimacy made her feel lonely, and she felt uncomfortable being a voyeur to love. She put her tinted windows up and finally removed her sunglasses.

I want to find somebody to fall in love with. She sighed and started her car. *Start with yourself,* her thoughts fired back. The response was so pervasive that it sounded as though something placed it in her head—like it wasn't even her thought! Despite having a fantastic morning, she found herself de-energized and depressed as she pulled out of the park.

WHILE ASHLEY NAVIGATED her way back home, Kerry-Ann was on her second hour at The Crown. Running the business from her initial takeover of the venue to seeing her first project come to life was grueling, but she managed on the strength of her love for the arts. She'd had to fight with folks who didn't want The Crown in the neighborhood and not lose her resolve from the stress of it all. Though her father didn't live in Atlanta and couldn't make it for her production, he did what he could from a distance: continued to encourage her to expand her dream and offered whatever financial assistance he could afford when she fell short.

"I know I don't say it often enough," he'd said to her on a call after her opening night, "but I have to tell you again that I am very proud of you, darling. I saw the pictures that you sent. It looked like everyone loved the show." Kerry-Ann had sent him screenshots of Tweets and other status updates from patrons who had mentioned *Corsets and Cognac* on social media after the first performance.

"Thank you, Daddy!" The words meant the world to her. He'd only started telling her how he felt after her mother passed away, so the words were soul-soothing to hear. She rarely, if ever, heard them as a child.

Errol was well into his 70's, and because of anxiety, did not like to travel. He needed structure and a strict routine to function well. Kerry-Ann only saw him when she went to Miami to visit. But he sent her cards, flowers, and even hand-written letters sometimes to keep in touch. Her father had not embraced texting—he would call her back after receiving messages instead of typing a reply—and barely grasped video calls. Instead of looking into the phone, he would answer it and set it down, so Kerry-Ann's view was of the ceiling instead of him.

After speaking with him, Kerry-Ann made her rounds to check on everything from the bar to the bathrooms. The feedback that she'd gotten from opening night had her running on a natural high. She was eager to build on that foundation of good energy and create something more outstanding for each audience during the run. That was the thing with live shows. No two nights are the same. Each was always an adventure.

The second and third nights were even more bold than before. The band was more in sync with the performers, and no cues were missed. Kerry-Ann became mythic. Iconic. Intense and wild. With her twirls, flips, spins, gymnast-like agility and grace, she enchanted the audience and Ashley alike. By the end of the second weekend of performances, the troupe had officially hit their stride. But one dancer, Felix, was annoyed at the growing closeness of Ashley and Kerry-Ann. He felt that she gave her more praise than the rest of them ever since he'd spied on them weeks before.

"Whew! I am starving," Kerry-Ann blurted out after a Sunday evening performance. "Y'all pack it up quickly so I can head out." She hurried the performers. Though Kerry-Ann felt great about her success, the long days were catching up to her and she needed to start having her last meal and getting to bed earlier if she was going to keep up the pace of managing The Crown.

"Where are you heading?" Ashley was curious.

Felix eyed them jealously, pulling another castmate aside to gossip and speculate.

"I'm gonna grab a bite at R. Thomas Grill. It's the only place I can count on to be open all night." Kerry-Ann spoke but her eyes looked beyond Ashley's shoulder to Felix whispering to Melanie. His body language was concerning, as their eyes met in a fleeting moment.

"I've heard of it but have never gone...been meaning to go after one of the shows, actually," Ashley noted.

Everyone began filing out and Kerry-Ann killed the lights. "Really great job tonight, everyone. Thanks so much!" She added as they scattered outside.

Ashley and Kerry-Ann walked to their cars. A silence loitered between them. Still wounded from her first advance being rebuffed,

Kerry-Ann decided against inviting Ashley to join her. "You should check it out sometime." She smiled politely.

Ashley clutched her keys and looked Kerry-Ann in the eyes apologetically. "Do you mind if I go with you tonight?"

The question severed the feelings of fatigue plaguing Kerry-Ann. A languid smile crept onto her face and a twinkle rose in her eyes. "Not at all. I'd love that."

"Great." Ashley was relieved that she hadn't made things awkward between them.

"You want to ride with me? Or do you want to drive yourself? I can bring you back to get your car if you'd like. Either way is fine." Kerry-Ann hoped she wasn't talking too much. She looked around the lot to see if anyone else was left. They weren't.

"I'll ride with you." Ashley surrendered in a sigh of relief. She was tired of wondering *what if*, as she had been doing since Kerry-Ann had asked her to lunch a few days ago. She'd had her reasons for wanting to stay away from women, but Ashley genuinely liked Kerry-Ann. *What's the worst that can happen?* She'd asked herself in the middle of a sleepless night. *Go for it if the opportunity comes up again.* That was the evening before, when her optimistic thoughts finally overpowered the pessimistic ones. Kerry-Ann's mention of dining— likely alone—was Ashley's sign to listen to her intuition and see what might happen. She went with it and hoped for the best.

R. Thomas Grill was a free-spirited eatery just ten minutes away from The Crown. Open 24/7, and enclosed in a giant tent, it was surrounded by plants, bird statues, and a host of colorful props. The menu was organic and vegan-friendly, tending to attract lots of folks in the entertainment industry, from small productions to celebrities involved in blockbuster films shooting across the city.

"Thanks for joining me," Kerry-Ann said as she navigated the short drive.

"You don't have to thank me. I wanted to."

"Well, I appreciate your presence. That's all. It'll be nice to wind down."

"Yeah..." Ashley bit her bottom lip. She unconsciously rubbed her hands together and cracked her knuckles.

There was a paid lot adjacent to the restaurant with lots of open spots when they arrived. As usual, there was a small crowd inside, but that didn't slow the service down. Once the ladies settled in with beverages and appetizers, their conversation flowed easily.

"You know, if someone would have told me five years ago that I'd be starring in a burlesque performance, I would have told them they were insane!"

"Didn't see it coming, huh?" Kerry-Ann giggled.

"Not at all! But I love it though. It's so...liberating. I *absolutely* love it!"

Kerry-Ann listened intently while picking at a beet salad. "Hm." She gazed at Ashley, grinning at the sight of her.

"What are you smiling at?"

"You. You're just so adorable."

Ashley blushed.

"I remember how much you resisted the idea of performing. How you foolishly felt self-conscious about your weight. As if there's anything not gorgeous about you," Kerry-Ann said matter-of-factly. "I'm inspired by you, Ashley."

"By *me*?" That was the last thing Ashley expected to hear.

"Yup. Most people wouldn't have taken the challenge. They wouldn't have overcome the self-confidence issues, but you did. And I admire that. It's a beautiful trait to have."

"Thank you! You are so full of compliments tonight! I don't even know what to say," Ashley spoke bashfully.

"Just receive them." Kerry-Ann winked.

Their waiter interrupted to bring out their main dishes. A portabella melt and sweet potato fries for Ashley and curry coconut seafood linguini for Kerry-Ann.

"I'm starving—gonna dig right in!" Kerry-Ann lit up at the sight of her plate.

As they dined, their chit chat quickly deviated from *Corsets and Cognac* to personal topics. Ashley admired Kerry-Ann's muscular shoulders and perfect posture even while seated.

"So, what made you decide to join me tonight?" Kerry-Ann built the courage to ask the question that had been pinging in her mind since they stood in The Crown's empty parking lot.

Ashley took a beat before responding. She swallowed and exhaled slowly. "Kerry-Ann, I wanted to join you the first time you asked me to. I was afraid, that's why I declined."

"Afraid of what?"

"I...I don't know. I guess—" She stuttered. "Not of you! I was unsure of how it would go because I've felt something with you in our performances. Something new. A different energy. And I didn't know if you felt it to. I didn't know if this would be a date or if I was way off base," Ashley poured her feelings out before she could talk herself out of being honest. If nothing else, she had made a promise to herself during the crumble of her marriage that she would never lie about her feelings again."

"Do you like it?"

"What?"

"The energy you feel between us."

Ashley froze. She lowered her gaze and pushed food around on her plate.

"Ouch," Kerry-Ann recoiled. "So that's a no," she assumed. Wounded again.

"No! It's not a no. I do enjoy it. It's all I can think about after we close each night. And the next morning."

Kerry-Ann relaxed into a smile. "Me too, and I did feel a shift. It was unexpected, but I embraced it. This is only a date if you want it to be."

"I don't know what I want. I just know that I'm nervous with women."

"I see," Kerry-Ann took a beat. "Have you ever dated one?"

"Yes." Ashley diverted her eyes and rubbed her neck.

Noticing her discomfort, Kerry-Ann backed off the topic. "So...

what do you like to do outside of dancing?" she smiled, hoping to steer the conversation back to a less threatening topic.

"Cook! That's actually what I do for a living. I still love it." She was grateful for the pivot.

"Oh really? What kind of chef are you?"

"Sushi. I do private catering for corporate events, mostly, but every now and then I'll do something special for couples."

"That sounds amazing. I'd love to try a meal if you're ever interested in making sushi for a party of one." Kerry-Ann couldn't help flirting again, entranced by Ashley's smile.

"I might be able to make an exception." Relaxed again, Ashley didn't mind the flirtatious banter. "I like you, Kerry-Ann," she affirmed. "And I'm sorry if I'm hard to read. It's just that I've made mistakes in my past and I don't want to repeat them. I'm afraid, especially when it comes to dating women."

"Why?"

Silence.

"It can't be that bad."

Still, a heavy reticence muted Ashley. Kerry-Ann picked up her cocktail with the palm of her hand and swirled it around before taking a slow sip.

"I don't mean to be rude. Really, I don't." Ashley felt guilty for her reservation.

"Then what is it?" Kerry-Ann instinctively placed her hand on Ashley's forearm, but soon pulled back.

"I'm so afraid of telling you the truth."

"You're safe with me—" Kerry-Ann began, but their words collided.

"Because that means bearing my soul and revealing my flaws. I'm petrified to tell you about my mistakes, "Ashley confessed.

"Whatever is in it can't be that bad. Plus, it's done," Kerry-Ann assured. "It shaped who you are today, and from where I sit, who you are is amazing."

Finally, Ashley met Kerry-Ann's gaze again. "Do you mind if we get the check and talk about it in the car? For a little more privacy?"

The restaurant had filled, and now other parties surrounded them on all sides.

"Of course. That's fine." Kerry-Ann quickly got the attention of their waiter and stealthily closed out their tab before Ashley could offer to pay.

"Thank you for that," Ashley spoke once they settled back in the vehicle. "For dinner, and for your patience."

"I just want you to be comfortable. Honestly, if you want me to take you back to your car, that's fine too."

"No, no! I want to be here with you. Right now. And I'm going to tell you why I said I was afraid."

"Okay."

Ashley stared forward—out of the windshield rather than face Kerry-Ann as she spoke. "I cheated," she huffed. "That's why I'm divorced. I cheated on my husband, and he couldn't get past the betrayal, so he left me." She blinked rapidly and fidgeted with her fingernails. Telling the truth was like poking an old wound. Though she thought she'd forgiven herself for sparking the demise of her marriage, the act of verbalizing it to a new love interest stung. She hadn't spoken about what happened for more than a year.

Kerry-Ann mulled over the admission. She nodded her head slowly and rubbed her chin. She leaned back before clearing her throat. "Okay, that's a start."

"Do you think that makes me a horrible person?" Ashley's gazed at Kerry-Ann timidly, a wave of shame.

"Without details," Kerry-Ann began. "I can't say. But knowing what I know about you so far, I'm going to guess that it doesn't. I think it makes you someone who made a mistake. I'm not even sure if I'd call it a mistake even though it certainly hurt everyone involved."

"Really?"

"Yes. I'm sure you have reasons why you did it," Kerry-Ann clarified. "And I believe that even though things fell apart, the fact that you risked it all to find something might mean that the break-up was necessary for you to be ultimately happy. It *might*. I could be completely wrong, but that's my first take at trying to understand."

"Wow," Ashley couldn't believe the grace with which Kerry-Ann spoke. "I won't excuse my behavior because it was wrong, and I could have done it all differently, but I did have reasons."

"Well, remember this. Whenever you're with me, you are in a safe space. A space created for authentic expression, even if it's painful."

Ashley drank Kerry-Ann's words.

"Do you want to tell me why you did it?"

"I do. But the truth is I'm terrified to go back to that time to reveal my flaws. To tell you about my mistakes. You seem so perfect and—"

"I'm not." Kerry-Ann swiftly corrected Ashley. "No one is."

"I know. It just feels like that sometimes. Anyway, I'll share," Ashley continued. "We were married for 16 years, and I loved him from the beginning to the end. A lack of love wasn't what caused me to do what I did."

"What was it?"

"Desperation, I guess you could say. To explore and define myself for myself."

Ashley rested her hand on the center console of Kerry-Ann's car. Kerry-Ann cautiously placed her palm on Ashley's wrist.

"I got married young," Ashley continued. "At twenty-two. Everything felt right, you know? Like we were following the path of our parents and everyone else: go to school, get a job, get married, start a family, blah, blah, blah."

Kerry-Ann listened intently, careful not to interrupt.

Ashley paused to sip from a bottle of water she'd had from earlier. "But I was always curious. For as long as I could remember, I was always attracted to women. Not as much as men, but still, I had the desire. And there was a long stretch of time where my husband wasn't attentive. All he cared about was work and earning more money."

"Sounds familiar."

"He traveled a lot. Didn't pay me much attention. Wasn't willing to listen when I tried to tell him about my feelings and curiosity," Ashley paused to catch her breath. "Despite loving each other, we fell out of sync."

"Hm."

"Then I met someone new. A woman who gave me everything that I'd yearned for. Attention. A feeling of safety to express myself. Nurturing. She did all of this without asking me for anything or pressuring me to be in a relationship. She was just there for me, and fell for her. I mean, I fell off a cliff!"

Kerry-Ann blocked the instinct to laugh at Ashley's emphasis.

"During one of my husband's getaways she and I met for dinner and a show at the Southwest Arts Center. Everything changed that night." Ashley took a rest.

"Take your time. I'm not in a hurry," Kerry-Ann processed all of the new information. The moment was tender, and she wanted Ashley to continue at the pace she needed to maintain comfort and honesty.

"We ended up back at her place after the show and...well, you know," Ashley didn't want to go into sexual details.

"I get it. You got physical."

"I'll never forget that experience for as long as I live. It was like being transported to an unearthly realm of pleasure, and afterwards, a part of me that hadn't relaxed in a long time finally gave way. Pressure, it vanished. But what replaced it was an emotional dumpster fire. It turns out we were both married. Had both cheated. And had both crossed a line we shouldn't have, not matter how good it felt. She had a wife. We were wrong."

Whew! Kerry-Ann's eyes widened, but she restrained her impulse reaction to speak. She hadn't seen all of this coming from Ashley yet kept her promise to be a safe space.

"So...that's the gist of it. He ultimately found out because I struggled with keeping my whereabouts a secret—I'd never had to. And after a while he noticed a pattern and used a GPS family-finder app on my phone that I'd forgotten was there to figure it all out."

"You kept sleeping with her?"

"No, but we met for dinner a few times after. They often lasted too long. Later than I'd ever usually been out for a meal with a friend."

"Mmm."

"I told him everything when shit hit the fan, and we tried to mend things through counseling. He admitted that he could have done a better job paying attention to me, but ultimately, I'd crushed his heart beyond repair, and I regret that deeply. All over a woman who wouldn't be there to help me pick up the pieces in the end. She's still with her wife."

"Damn. Now I understand why you declined my first invitation."

"Yes." Ashley's heart pounded. "I don't know if you've ever been through a divorce, but it was the most scarring event of my life. Emotionally, psychologically, spiritually, financially—in every way that you could think of, it devastated me, especially since I'd done it to myself. Little things like getting his mail after he'd moved out or going grocery shopping for two instead of three brought me to tears. The pain of losing the respect of my son crushed me—his dad had told him what happened."

Kerry-Ann sighed. She could feel Ashley's hurt as she told the story.

"For a long time, I felt like my life was over," Ashley went on, tears welling in her eyes. "I was deathly afraid to talk to women, even when I was ready to date again because in my mind, my having been inti- mate with a woman is what caused all the pain in my family. And I never wanted to go through that again. I know it's irrational, but that's what my mind did with the outcome of that situation."

"I hear you. Even though I've never been in your shoes, I'll tell you what I do know," Kerry-Ann said. "And that is, it takes a lot of courage to live true to yourself. To live a life designed by you and not by others. I know that it takes strength to admit you were wrong and the cause of your marriage ending. It shows growth to go from who you were then to who you are now."

"Thank you for not judging me." Ashley's fingers trembled against the console.

A silence fell over the women. Kerry-Ann stared straight ahead, her fingers tapping the steering wheel. Ashley's confession was a lot to take in. "How long ago did all of this happen?" She wanted to know why her gut didn't tell her to flee. Kerry-Ann never realized she could be so understanding.

"Three years ago. It feels like a lifetime now, finally. So...that's it. I've told you about my issues. My wounds were self-inflected. I was afraid to share because you seem so perfect. So together. Everything I'm not."

"Perfect? Me? Ha!"

"Do you wish you never asked me out?" Ashley felt sweat bead up at her temple. She crossed her legs and folded her arms.

"I believe that there is a reason for everything," Kerry-Ann began. "Even if the things we do have the worst timing or break the hearts of the ones we love, there's always a reason why. Because I don't' think people intentionally hurt the ones they love. The pain is a result of them trying to figure out how to love themselves while feeling confined." Kerry-Ann surprised herself.

"I wanted a taste of freedom and I couldn't get it within the boundaries of my marriage. Ended up hurting myself in the worst way imaginable."

"But did you get your freedom?"

"I did. I don't know if it was worth the cost."

"I see." Kerry-Ann drank in Ashley's words. "I was married once, too."

Ashley's head spun. Her mouth fell open.

"My wife and I grew apart over time," Kerry-Ann continued. "We probably could have worked harder to make it work, but the time for great communication in a relationship is the beginning, not the end. By then it's almost always too late."

"Tell me about it."

They exhaled in unison.

"Thankfully," Kerry-Ann continued. "She and I had as stress-free of a split as possible. We were cordial despite everything we'd built unraveling. It still hurt like hell though."

"When was that?"

"Four years ago." Kerry-Ann huffed out a puff of air. "Feels like ten," she chuckled nervously. "I guess that's why I was able to listen to your confession with empathy and ease."

"But *you* didn't cheat."

"I didn't, no. But in the years after my divorce, I did a lot of searching and inner work. Asked a lot of questions."

"Like what?"

"Like if divorce really meant failure? And if so, says who? Why does the end mean a fail? What if it simply ended because it was time and not all relationships are supposed to be for a lifetime?"

"That's not what we were taught."

"But why do we cling to those rules? In every other area of our lives—like jobs, careers, or houses or what art we like, or books we read—we acknowledge that our preferences change and evolve. That perfection isn't possible. But when it comes to marriage that thinking goes out the window."

"True..."

"Some of my friends told me I was being selfish and making a mistake leaving my ex, but I wanted out. It had run its course and I was okay with that."

"I wish it were that easy for me. I always thought I had to make it to the end. To celebrate 50 plus years like older people have done."

"I feel like we compare ourselves to grandparents who lived in completely different cultural times. We ignore the reality that them staying together for 50 years didn't always mean they were happy the whole time. Didn't mean that affairs didn't happen, but maybe our mothers couldn't afford to leave. And even if she could, it wasn't socially acceptable for her to do so. So, folks stayed together for a lot of reasons, and a lot of them probably weren't happiness. Just my thoughts though."

Now Ashley was speechless.

"I'm not making excuses for infidelity and people who intentionally hurt others for selfish reasons. Like you said, you were still wrong but...your husband admitted to dropping the ball too, so..."

"Yeah." Ashley glanced at Kerry-Ann, feeling the safe space Kerry-Ann had spoken of. Their conversation caused a weight-lifting shift in her. "Thank you. For everything tonight. I know I talked your ear off."

"I wanted to hear your story. I'm glad I did."

They exhaled. The night ended up lasting much longer than either of them had planned. Soon, Kerry-Ann drove Ashley back to The Crown to get her car. Their parting was quiet and dotted only by a light hug. Despite the brutal honesty of the evening, Ashley felt relieved. She didn't know what step they would take next outside of the show, but she was grateful for the space and friendship that Kerry-Ann had given her that night.

As she pulled out of the lot, Kerry-Ann noticed a bright orange notice on the front door of The Crown. She drove up to it and was severely disappointed to find that it was an anonymous message to not "bring immoral smut" to Virginia Highlands. "Great. Like I need to deal with this shit." She flung the paper in the trash and drove home.

CHAPTER 6

The next night, Ashley and Kerry-Ann set the stage on fire. They were more in sync. More submerged in their act than any other performance. The women moved like water. Fluid. Free. Beautifully intertwining. They flowed. Their cage scene intensified, lifting them into a mantle of unfiltered sensuality. Kerry-Ann had to catch her breath.

While the two women arguably had their best night, there was a noticeable difference in the energy of the rest of the group. Felix was off. He missed cues and didn't seem to care. Kerry-Ann didn't know what was going on with him. A firm believer in being straightforward, she approached him privately before he left for the night.

An athletic dancer with ballet training, Felix was usually the quietest in the troupe. "Felo?" Kerry-Ann called him by his nickname. She wanted to start the conversation as disarmingly as possible.

He smiled at the sound of his name rolling off her lips.

"Hey Kerry-Ann. What's up?" He cleared his throat.

"Not much. I just wanted to check in with you. See how you were feeling with the show. If there's anything you need?"

"Oh, I'm fine." Felix glanced at the floor.

She touched his hand. "You sure? Seemed liked you were having an off night tonight."

"Oy. You noticed..." He raised his eyes to meet her. Gently pulling his hand from hers. He sighed and folded his arms, squeezing his biceps. "I'm okay. Really. It happens, know?"

"Did something happen? Anything I should know about?" She nodded affirmatively, a very subtle motion prompting him to concede."

"Nothing happened, Kerry-Ann. It's just...it's Ashley."

"Ashley?" The name was unexpected.

"I feel like you two...you know...are closer than the rest of us. Like you pay more attention to her than anybody else."

"Well, I have more scenes with her."

His jaw tightened. "Yeah...I know."

Something clicked. Kerry-Ann wondered if Felix had had a crush on her. The emphasis he put on the word "know" was unmistakable, as if it irritated him. "Okay. I hear you. And I'm sorry that you feel that way."

"It's not a big deal, sorry," he tried to save face with a lackluster apology.

Kerry-Ann straightened her posture and looked him in the eyes. "I appreciate everybody making this show a reality. Every night we make magic—together—as a group, no one contributing any more or less than anybody else. I'm very proud of what you bring, Felo. And the audience loves you!" She placated him while trying to figure out how else to nip any jealousy in the bud.

"Thank you. I apologize for not giving it my all tonight."

"Felix, did you do that intentionally?"

"No! I don't think so," He grimaced. "It won't happen again."

Kerry-Ann studied him, nothing that she'd have to dial back with Ashley when around them. She didn't think she was overt.

"You got my word." His voice weakened, embarrassed.

"It's okay. Like you said, off nights happen, right? I meant what I said though. I really appreciate you. And if you ever need anything just let me know and I'll try my best to get it for you. We're a team."

"Thank you."

"Alright. I know you were leaving so I won't hold you up," Kerry-Ann transitioned the conversation. "Have a good night."

"Good night." Pensive, he left.

Kerry-Ann ran her hands over her head and tilted it upward as if waiting for a sign to fall from above. If she was right about Felix, his emotions could complicate things. Even if she was wrong, her conversation with him reminded her of a need for discretion with Ashley when others were might be around. Kerry-Ann didn't need anything threatening the success and professionalism of the show. "Fuck..." she remembered thinking it was a bad idea to approach Ashley outside of the context of the show and platonic friendship, but she couldn't help it. She was drawn to her. Now Kerry-Ann would have to be much more careful about their moments together.

"Hey!" Ashley hadn't been far away and witnessed a part of Kerry-Ann's exchange with Felix. She'd seen her take him by the hand. "What's going on?"

Kerry-Ann tapped her side instinctively. Nerves.

"Just checking in with Felix."

"Everything okay?" Ashley looked her in the eyes.

"Uh, yeah. Everything is fine. He was just having an off night." She debated telling Ashley her suspicion, but decided not to in case she was wrong and in the event they weren't as alone as they thought they were. "Do you mind hanging around for a bit? I need to make rounds really quick, but I want to spend some time with you off the clock."

"That's fine." Ashley felt that something wasn't right but didn't know what. She hoped she wasn't making a mistake.

"I'll be right back."

You should leave. Ashley ignored her gut feeling and ambled back out to the stage while Kerry-Ann disappeared into the venue. It felt like she'd been gone a long time before she re-appeared with a look of relief on her face. No one else was in the building. She'd done a walk-through and checked the security cameras.

"Sorry about that. I just wanted to make sure we were alone. That no one else could eavesdrop on our conversation or see us."

Ashley's shoulders gave way. Privacy. "Ah, I see." She smiled broadly. "Thank you for thinking of it! I'm usually much better at discretion."

Unlike the previous evening, there wasn't a lot of dialog. Ashley gazed at Kerry-Ann as they sat on the edge of the stage, desire leaping from her eyes. Kerry-Ann's mature response to Ashley's past was a needle that pierced the cloud of fear in which Ashley had shrouded herself. She admired every detail of Kerry-Ann's face. From a tiny scar above her upper lip to eyes the color of deliciously aged brandy, Kerry-Ann beguiled. Her skin still shimmered with body glitter from the show, but more than her physicality, Ashley was drawn to the totality of Kerry-Ann's being. She reached for her hand.

"I enjoyed tonight," Ashley confessed. "A lot."

"I'm glad. So did I."

Ashley inched closer and exhaled. She closed her eyes, unsure of what to do next. Kerry-Ann rested a hand on Ashley's knee and inched closer. She gently ran her fingertips across Ashley's skin until Ashley opened her eyes and faced her. They shared a glance before Ashley finally leaned forward for a timid kiss. It was slow, and her lips trembled after making contact with Kerry-Ann's. Sinking into the moment, Kerry-Ann squeezed Ashley's thigh with one hand and cupped her face for a deeper kiss. A thrilling moan escaped Ashley. It had been years since she kissed another woman. Their soft pecks soon turned to a ravishing kiss.

Ashley went adrift in the moment but was jolted out of it by the vibration of her phone next to her on the stage. The women broke away with girlish smiles. Ashley glanced at her illuminated device. It was her son. She debated answering it but decided against it. She would call him back later. This was her time. Under spell from the intimacy with Kerry-Ann, Ashley fought hard to suppress a tremor of desire that rippled over her.

"Your lips are just as soft as I imagined they would be." Kerry-Ann eyed Ashley with a confidence that destroyed all resistance, but she didn't advance. She allowed her statement to linger.

"Thank you." Ashley didn't know if that was the right response, but it was the first one to come to mind. Heat rushed to her sacral chakra, seeped down to her entire sexual region. Desire pumped blood through her thighs. A slow pulse beat between her legs.

Kerry-Ann smiled and backed off. "You're so attractive." She tapped the stage and began standing up. Although she wanted to get swept away in the tenderness of the moment, Kerry-Ann kept her desires at bay. "Why don't I walk you to your car?"

Ashley was confused. She hadn't expected the quick pivot. "Oh—okay." She didn't know what to say, so she followed Kerry-Ann's lead.

It wasn't that Kerry-Ann wanted to leave, she needed to be sure she wasn't rushing and would do anything with Ashley that might complicate their relationship or the show. Kerry-Ann had gone over everything she'd learned about Ashely and her past. Even though she understood why she cheated and didn't want to be a hypocrite, and act as though *she'd* never made mistakes, Kerry-Ann still wanted to give Ashley time to make sure being with a woman was something she wouldn't again regret. Kerry-Ann didn't want to get hurt either.

DAYS later they found themselves alone again for Sunday brunch at Livingston Bar and Restaurant, a gorgeous downtown hotel eatery with a luxurious setting. The energy between them flowed smoothly, neutralized of angst on both sides. While they dined, and chatted, and drank alcohol-free beverages, Kerry-Ann and Ashley sank into a mutual desire and fascination with one another. By the time the check arrived, they once again were holding hands. A crack of thunder outside prompted them to leave sooner than they'd planned.

"Good thing we had valet parking," Ashley nodded outside. The rain started slowly at first, but quickly turned into a deluge.

"I know!" Kerry-Ann stood up and pushed her chair in. "We would have gotten soaked walking to our cars."

Ashley glanced up, unexpectedly titillated by Kerry-Ann's word choice. She stared, intrigued and half smiling as she got up. "Well, you don't have to worry about getting *too* wet."

Electricity. They both felt it. Kerry-Ann smirked. "Hm."

They walked toward the exit. "Unless you want to." The words lurched out of Ashley's mouth before she could barricade them.

"What?"

Ashely took a jaggedly deep breath. "Get wet..."

Kerry-Ann raised an eyebrow, connecting the dots to Ashley's naughty gaffe. "I don't mind. I want to, but...do you?"

Ashley bit her bottom lip. "Yes." She didn't want to fight it anymore. She didn't want to delay pleasure any longer. She didn't want to deny her cravings. She was ready to dive back into sleeping with a woman. "Yes," Ashley repeated as the valet pulled around in her car. "I'll text you my address."

A devilish grin crept onto Kerry-Ann's face. Less than thirty minutes later the women were pressed against each other in a ravenous clutch. Kerry-Ann kicked off her shoes in Ashley's foyer and they melted into each other like swollen rain clouds ready to burst. Kissing. Groping. Moaning.

"Mm. Oh God..." Ashley stole a moment to catch her breath. She hadn't been so aroused in years. "Come in." She paced herself. "Let me get you something to drink. You can relax on any of the chairs."

"Thank you." Kerry-Ann was grateful for the pause but knew it wouldn't last long.

"Water, wine, lemonade?"

"Lemonade is fine."

"Gotcha." Ashley stole a moment to regroup. "Do you have any food allergies or anything that you hate, by the way?"

"No allergies. I'm pretty open-minded. Not big on salmon, but that's about it. Why?"

"I just figured since you're here, maybe I can prepare a quick meal for you. If you want." Girlish excitement fluttered in Ashley once again.

"Oh, you want to bring out *Chef* Ashley, I see," Kerry-Ann teased. "I would love that." She grinned.

"Coming right up." She glinted and only paused to grab her phone to trigger music through a built-in surround sound system.

"May I use your bathroom?" Kerry-Ann wanted to freshen up.

"Of course. It's that door right there," Ashley pointed to a door behind Kerry-Ann.

Prepped sushi ingredients were already in the fridge, which made it easy for Ashley to whip up something she hoped would be impressive. Soon after placing Kerry-Ann's glass of lemonade on the table, Ashley busied herself making an "Avocado Bomb" appetizer—fresh avocado stuffed with spicy crab and tuna flash-fried in tempura.

Kerry-Ann returned and glanced around the home while Ashley worked in the kitchen. Tidy. A few pictures of Ashley and her son, a few with two dogs—from puppies to seniors. Fresh flowers on the end tables. It was inviting. She noticed the drink on the kitchen table and took the cue to take a seat there.

Ashley topped off the first course with spicy mayo and eel sauce. She grabbed a white plate to place on a gold table charger before inviting Kerry-Ann to try it.

"Chopsticks or flatware?"

"Flatware, thank you. I'm not very good at using chopsticks."

"No worries at all." Ashley pulled out a gorgeous gold and malachite knife and fork set. "Here you go. This is a starter." Ashley stood patiently. Optimistically.

"Ooh!" Kerry-Ann's eyes lit up at first bite. "This is delicious!" She licked her lips in self-awareness, hoping no sauce was there.

"Thank you! I've got something else coming up for you. You enjoy that for now."

Kerry-Ann blushed. *She's cooking for me!*

Ashley worked quickly in the kitchen as she wanted the timing of the next tasting to be perfect. She turned her prep ingredients into a Spider Roll with fried softshell crab, avocado, asparagus, bell peppers and shredded crab meat wrapped in seaweed and black sushi rice. Kerry-Ann looked on in amazement at how effortlessly Ashley moved about her kitchen. She paced herself eating the Avocado bomb because she could sense Ashley's intent to work expeditiously. Just as Kerry-Ann was nearing her last bite Ashley began using a combination of soy sauce, sriracha and wasabi to make an elegant tree design on a large white plate. Once finished with the art, she placed the Spider roll strategically at the center.

"Here is your personal roll. I know you may not be hungry enough to eat it all right now, but you can at least take a bite or two."

"Ashley, this is so creative! How did you do this so fast?"

"I can't tell you my tricks now, can I?" Ashley chuckled and took a seat next to her. She shared the list of ingredients with Kerry-Ann before letting her taste it.

"It's so pretty. I feel like I should take a picture of it!" Kerry-Ann was impressed.

"You can if you'd like," Ashley chuckled, "but hopefully, there will be more times."

Kerry-Ann couldn't help herself. She snapped a photo of her meal. And another of a bashful Ashley.

"Would you like me to feed it to you?"

The question excited Kerry-Ann. She nodded yes, unable to speak.

Ashley made a quick movement to get up and grab a fresh set of chopsticks before returning to the table. "Normally, I would never cut a roll with a knife, but I think to make it easier for you to bite, I should make an exception." She first sliced a roll in half and then used chopsticks to feed Kerry-Ann a manageable-sized piece. Kerry-Ann closed her eyes in delight as she tasted the roll. Ashley slowly pulled the sticks out of her mouth.

"Mm. That was just tasty as the appetizer," Kerry-Ann confessed. "Why don't you let me feed you the other half since you did all the work to cook?"

"I'd like that."

Kerry-Ann picked up the other half of the roll and gently brought it to Ashley's lip waiting lips. Ashley's tongue grazed the tips of Kerry-Ann's fingertips as she pulled the sushi into her mouth.

"Oh, these definitely taste better when fed by you," she said after eating it.

"Thank you so much for this. I really wasn't expecting it." Ashley was grateful for the impromptu gesture.

"It was more than a pleasure. I'm excited to be with you." A moment of silence lingered between them before Ashley suggested they relax on the couch a bit. She'd covered up the uneaten food and wanted to unwind. "Bring your drink," she suggested and poured a glass for herself.

Placing both drinks on coasters, Ashley gently touched one of Kerry-Ann's legs. "How about a foot rub?"

"I will never turn that down!"

Ashley winked. *What dancer would?*

"Mmm," Kerry-Ann was shocked at Ashley's skill. Her fingertips felt like well-trained deliverers of pleasure. She hit pressure points and seemed to know exactly where to touch to arouse sensation. Her skills were courtesy of taking lessons for personal enrichment. Ashley's ex-husband would always complain of sore muscles, so she'd decided to learn how to give proper massages to soothe him.

Ashley moved to Kerry-Ann's calves, taking her time to knead and soothe tension away. She relaxed her body, quieted both their minds and instinctively guided them into a sweeping rhythm of exploration. And natural inclination. In the moment, Kerry-Ann felt the relinquishing of control—an emotional surrender that was long overdue.

"Your touch feels so amazing. It's a gift I didn't know that I needed. Thank you," Kerry-Ann spoke. "I admit that I didn't see this coming either."

"What's that?"

"You taking the lead."

Ashley laughed. "Neither did I!"

"It's different for me. I like it." Kerry-Ann descended into relaxation, welcoming Ashley's slow awakening of her body. "Please, don't stop."

Ashley was pleasantly surprised that Kerry-Ann allowed herself to receive pleasure without rushing to try and reciprocate. She wasn't

used to it. Kerry-Ann's yielding, her way of letting Ashley deliver grat-
ification without rushing to do it in returned signified confidence.
Power. Kerry-Ann's behavior was hypnotic. Her assured responses to
everything seemed so developed and advanced that she was sure to
be a taste of paradise, Ashley presumed.

Twenty minutes would pass before layers of clothing came off. By
then, Kerry-Ann was ready to give back. Her body was awake, alive,
open and eager to exchange energy. She climbed on top of Ashley,
kissing her earlobes, biting her neck and exploring the curves and
creases of her body. Desire pulsed through the room like a neo-soul
bassline. The flesh of their yonis swelled with anticipation and
dripped with eagerness. The first orgasm came without any major
skin friction. Ashley was shocked. Her climax was so subtle and
sneaky that it glided over her like windblown waves whisking across
water's surface. Kerry-Ann had rubbed her thumbs over Ashley's
nipples, cupped her breasts like sweet, small fruit. Licked them gently
for ample time before sucking them. She'd kissed around the edges
of Ashley's chest, down her sides, all over her stomach and blew a
gentle breeze of breath across her skin.

Kerry-Ann had grabbed a firm hold of Ashley's hips, kissed
around her pelvic bone. She licked the tiny trail of hair that decorated Ashley's stomach while sliding her right hand down to palm
her pussy. She held it, closing her eyes to submerge into the feeling of
Ashley's sticky wetness oozing onto her hands. Eventually, Kerry-Ann
used two fingers to trace Ashley's vulva, the edges of her lips, her
labia and gently she probed just inside Ashley's opening. There,
Kerry-Ann lingered, meandering in the heat of Ashley's gateway,
swirling her slick fingers around to discover where Ashley was most
sensitive. Their moans grew. Their desire was high. Ashley began to
seep ecstasy, coating Kerry-Ann's hand with her juices. Kerry-Ann
slowed down to a crawl, pulled out and looked at Ashely. Without a
blink or hesitation, she placed the finger that she'd pulled out of
Ashley into her mouth. She sucked it and ran her tongue over it as
though she were playing with a cherry stem.

"I love the way you taste." She kissed her way back to Ashley's breasts, continuing to play with them and arouse her to a shuddering climax.

"Whew...I—um—Kerry-Ann—" Ashley lost her words.

She hadn't experienced an orgasm like that in her life. She could only describe it to herself as beautifully jarring. Even though she'd set the tone for the afternoon, somehow Kerry-Ann commanded that moment.

A mutual exchange of bliss punctuated the next two hours as they moved from the couch to Ashley's bedroom.

"Shower?" Ashley invited Kerry-Ann into her large master suite.

"Oh, yes."

Ashley's bathroom looked like heaven. The walls shimmered with gold wallpaper and candles were everywhere. Kerry-Ann giggled.

"What?"

"I like your style. Reminds me of The Crown."

"Ha! Great minds think alike, I guess?" She blew Kerry-Ann a kiss. "You'll probably really like this then," Ashley said. With one flick of a switch, an electric shade slid down to block out the sun. She pushed a button and a strip of electric candles lit up.

"I do," Kerry-Ann beamed. She was ready to ravage her.

Ashley turned on the shower, grabbed two towels and shower caps. She took a moment to embrace Kerry-Ann while waiting for the water to get to a comfortable temperature. Ashley nibbled on Kerry-Ann's neck and shoulders before finally opening the shower door and inviting her to step in. On the sink counter, her phone lit up silently. It was her son again, but Ashley hadn't noticed. In the shower, the women picked up where they'd left off on the sofa, bathing each other in vanilla-pineapple body scrub. With their eyes, hands, lips and tongues, they feasted on each other, both reaching another rousing climax, this time simultaneously cumming under the water-fall of warm water. They nearly buckled from the intensity.

"I need to lay down," Kerry-Ann admitted.

"Me too." Ashley's orgasm was an explosion of ecstasy. Despite the water, she could feel sexual fluids pooling between her thighs. Kerry-Ann had penetrated her slowly, searching inside for spots of heightened sensitivity all while her thumb massaged Ashley's clit and they kissed. "Oh, fuck..." she trembled. "Come. Follow me."

Ashley handed Kerry-Ann a towel and took her by the hand, leading her to her queen bed where they collapsed on violet and gold sheets. Surrounded by brocade pillows with tassels and fringe, they lay naked in each other's arms. Kerry-Ann kissed Ashley's hand and forehead as they basked without need for conversation. Music wafted in from the lower level of Ashley's home. R&B. The moment was temperate. Beautiful. Revitalizing and sensational.

"Kerry-Ann?" Ashley wasn't sure if she'd dozed off. She whispered her name.

Kerry-Ann stirred. She had fallen asleep. "Hm?" She gathered herself. Smiled a little and sniffled as if that would bring her out of drowsiness faster.

Ashley giggled. "Sorry, I hope I didn't disrupt your peace."

"You gave me peace."

Kerry-Ann's words made Ashley's heart skip a beat. "Thank you. And thank you for taking a chance with me. For coming over."

"I would be lying if I said I hadn't fantasized sharing a moment like this with you for a long time now."

"Oh, the pressure! I hope I lived up to your dreams."

"You were beyond my wildest daydreams. I didn't know what to expect, but I can assure you, I am *not* disappointed."

"Whew!" Ashley feigned relief. "Well, I'm processing, but it's a good process. I feel lighter. A bit surer of myself."

"Tell me more."

"About my sexuality, you know? Like all the time I spent running away from my desires would have been better spent figuring out how to love myself."

"You still have a lot of time left." Kerry-Ann looked Ashley directly in the eyes. Again, a hush fell over them.

The ladies would nap, take a mini food break, and light one more fuse of intimacy before Kerry-Ann peeled herself away. They didn't have to talk a lot. Energy flowed seamlessly between them. Neither felt unsure, nor had regrets for stepping over the line from friendship to lovers. Over the next few days, they would converse and indulge one another sexually as often as possible. They had to work harder at not letting their new love affair spill over into their performance too much. But things didn't always go so smoothly. More than once they were nose-to-nose in the cage and struggled to keep from progressing to a kiss. Hiding their affair was too hard and Kerry-Ann worried that Felix would catch their lingering stares and cause trouble. With just another week before the show was scheduled to close, Kerry-Ann had to come clean about the feeling she had about Felix liking her and why it was critical that she and Ashley tone down their true desires while on stage.

"Why didn't you tell me at the time?" Ashley felt slighted.

"I didn't want it to be true, but I feel like it is. He hasn't confessed or anything. I just feel it."

Ashley was silent.

"I'm sorry. I was just trying to avoid making it a big deal."

"Do you like him?"

"What? Absolutely not. I am a whole entire lesbian and have *no* interest in Felix."

"But I saw you...I saw you holding his hand..."

Kerry-Ann's shoulders dropped. "That night? You were watching?"

"Not intentionally! I was looking for you and stumbled into where you guys were. I backed off after sensing the mood of the moment. It was none of my business, really. You and I aren't... you know," Ashley cut herself off from rambling.

"Ashley, I promise that was nothing. I was trying to put him at ease because I knew he was upset but not telling me why."

"So, you held his hand like a child?"

"Like someone who needed comfort to tell the truth. Just like I did with you." A heavy silence infiltrated their dialog before Kerry-Ann continued. "Except, I am so into you that it scares me."

Ashley exhaled loudly, wanting to believe Kerry-Ann, but struck by fear.

"All I'm asking is that we keep things between us quiet until we close out next week. I can only manage so much at a time, Ash, please."

Ash. She noted Kerry-Ann's shortening of her name. The simple utterance softened her. "I get it. And I'm nervous too."

"I do want you, and I don't want to hide. I just think it's best for right now.

"You're right. It's early, and we shouldn't let others catch on," Ashley gave in. "There's too much at stake and we need to keep it professional."

"We do."

Ashley felt rusty at dating and was glad they were able to cross that moment with pure honesty. It was another thing she needed to get used to. Lowering her defenses and she says what was on her mind. Kerry-Ann was already making a great impact on her as a person.

CHAPTER 7

Corsets and Cognac was drawing near the close of a two-month run, having flourished from an embryo of an idea in Kerry-Ann's mind to a full-scale performance that proved itself every night with audiences. Kerry-Ann felt bittersweet about her first production nearing its end—thrilled that even with hiccups and mishaps throughout its run, the size of her audience grew. The experience was everything she'd ever wanted, yet she was nervous about having to do it all over again soon with a new show. Next time, she'd have an assistant artistic director to shoulder the burden of managing all of the creative aspects of launching a new vision.

Ashley. She had become emboldened in her self-expression, both on the stage and off. Yet, there were some nights when Ashley admitted she didn't feel like doing the show—experiencing general fatigue, not feeling sexy, and bloated. Kerry-Ann had warned her about those days back when they were rehearsing. It was on an evening like this that Ashley and Kerry-Ann had their first *off* performance. Were it not for Kerry-Ann improvising on the fly, one of their scenes would have been unflatteringly wrong due to Ashley missing several transitions.

"Sorry about that tonight," Ashley felt sorry for throwing their routine off.

Kerry-Ann huffed, but kept her response positive. "It happens. Don't worry about it." Kerry-Ann had been nervous and annoyed when Ashley slipped up, but she also knew that she'd had her fair share of missed cues and missteps herself while under the spotlight.

The truth was they were both tired. Ashley still worked as a full-time chef during the day and playing phone tag with her son while Kerry-Ann took care of the business end of running an adult entertainment establishment. She'd had her fair share of residents objecting to The Crown's location, but thankfully, those who loved her club outnumbered those who did not. Together, Kerry-Ann and Ashley were juggling myriad responsibilities and emotions. Hiding their love affair from the cast also put pressure on them—Felix ended up not being a problem at all. All the while though, their infatuation with one another grew by the day. They'd gone out several times on their off days...to Stone Mountain to hike, to the botanical garden to admire topiary installations, and even up to the Trap Music Museum to check out hip hop's early history. Things were going well on all accords until Ashley got the shock of a lifetime.

"Excuse me, Kerry-Ann," Ashley spoke earnestly on the eve of the final show. She was at Kerry-Ann's condo when three successive calls from her son came through. "David. What's up?" she answered.

"Mom! Where have you been? I've been calling you," David admonished. His voice quavered.

Ashley sat up. "I know. I called you back! Why didn't you just leave a message or text what you needed."

"I didn't want to text you. Not for this.

Ashley's nerves woke up. "What's going on?"

"It's Dad."

She gulped, standing up and walking away from Kerry-Ann. "What about him? What's the matter?"

Kerry-Ann looked on, concerned.

It's okay, Ashley mouthed while raising a hand to Kerry-Ann. Her stomach told her she was wrong, but she didn't want to alarm Kerry-Ann.

"He's too stubborn to tell you this, Mom. And I've been respecting his privacy, so I haven't told you either. But I don't think it's right that you don't know," David took a labored breath. "Dad has leukemia. They're saying he's only got six months to live."

"Oh, David," Ashley was blindsided.

"And his girlfriend left him. Said she doesn't want to be anybody's nurse."

Bitch. Ashley's thought appeared in her head like sorcery. She hadn't spoken to her ex-husband in months and her son didn't call as much as he used to. Still, she thought it cruel to leave someone with that kind of prognosis. "What do you want me to do? He doesn't want to speak to me."

From these questions, Kerry-Ann figured out who the call was about. She stared at Ashley curiously, but held back other reactions.

"Call him anyway," David begged. "Please. I don't want him to be alone. I'm trying to figure out how I can be there for him and finish school." David was a junior at Appalachian State University in Boone, NC.

Ashley's belly turned. She slid into a swivel chair next to the sofa on which Kerry-Ann patiently waited. "All right. I'll call him," Ashley relented. She felt as though she'd been dropkicked off cloud nine. "How are you otherwise?" she quizzed her son.

"I'm okay, I guess." A silence roved through their conversation.

"All right...do you need anything?"

"No," he answered swiftly. "Well," David spoke again. "Mom, we should talk. Not right now. But soon."

The words put fear in Ashley's heart. She didn't know what else he could say to her that he hadn't already said. David never forgave her for breaking up their family. He'd grown more cordial and respectful again after the second year, but their relationship had never been the same.

"About what?" she pressed him.

"I need to find a way to make things right with you. This...whole situation with dad made me rethink stuff. Like, maybe I should stop holding grudges against you. I don't know."

Tears ran down Ashley's face. She wished she were alone but had had so much of the conversation already in front of Kerry-Ann she felt it odd that she excuse herself now. Besides, she ached for comfort. Her stomach was in knots. "Okay, I understand. I'd love that." Her tears were a mixture of relief, joy, grief, and sorrow. "I gotta go, son. Thanks for calling me." She needed to unpack her emotions. "And we'll definitely have that talk. I love you."

"Love you too, Mom."

Ashley told Kerry-Ann everything. She shared her fear of reaching out to her ex-husband. She didn't know what to expect from the call. Would he tell her to go to hell? Would he remind her how much he hated her? Would he pick up the phone at all?

"I hope this doesn't make things uncomfortable between us," Ashley said.

Kerry-Ann's leg shook nervously. "It won't if we don't make it." She hoped Ashley's past wouldn't threaten their future. Kerry-Ann had really fallen for her over the last couple of months. "How do you feel about him?"

"Huh?"

"Your husband. Do you still love him?"

"I don't hate him."

Nervousness ricocheted in Kerry-Ann's chest.

"But I'm certainly not in love with him. Absolutely not. He's the father of my child. I'll always have a little love for him even if he hates me. But it isn't the same energy of love that I feel for you."

Kerry-Ann's mouth fell open. She wasn't sure she'd heard Ashley right. "Are you saying that you..."

There were too many emotions. Ashley wanted to ratify, *yes, I love you,* but didn't want to rush. Didn't want to confuse great sex and awesome conversation with love.

"That if I'm not already there, I'm certainly falling," Ashley confirmed. She looked up and through her fear. "In love. Yes." Ashley was scared shitless. She couldn't believe she came out and said it.

"With me?"

"Of course!"

Kerry-Ann's foolish question broke the tension in the room. Ashley got up and moved back to her side on the couch.

"Don't feel like you need to say it back if you're not there yet," Ashley said. "If there's one thing I've learned it's to only say what you mean and mean what you say."

"It's okay. I'm not afraid to admit that I've fallen in love with you one hour at a time over the course of this year. Since the day you walked into my class, I've felt drawn to you. I had to keep boundaries and remain professional. But Ashley, I've got to tell you, the last few months getting closer to you have been the most exhilarating of my life. I am definitely am in love with you. *And* I'm scared!"

"Shit. Me too."

"But if we continue the way we've been. Open. Honest. Vulnerable, and willing to talk through anything. I think we can get through this...whatever it ends up meaning for you."

"Do you really mean that?"

"Yes, I do."

"Oh, Kerry-Ann..." more tears formed in Ashley's eyes.

Kerry-Ann pulled her close and encouraged Ashley to cry. To release all the pain and shame that had lodged itself in her. "Let it all out. You don't have room for it anymore. Love needs space to grow."

The women cradled each other for a little while longer before Ashley prepared to leave. As much as she'd like to spend the night in Kerry-Ann's bed, she had an early start the next morning. She also didn't want Kerry-Ann to spend the night before their final show thinking about the new challenge in their relationship.

Kerry-Ann walked Ashley to her car in the driveway.

"Let's make tomorrow night the most amazing performance of the entire run," Ashley said before leaving. "I'll be there 100% regardless of whatever else is going on. I don't want you to worry about me being distracted. I won't be!"

"Thank you. I wasn't thinking about that but I appreciate that you were. Don't worry, babe. We'll navigate everything. I'm sure of it. Good night." Before retreating inside, Kerry-Ann leaned down for one last kiss as Ashley met her lips.

THE FINAL PRESENTATION of *Corsets and Cognac* played to a sold-out crowd. True to her words the evening before, Ashley did not let the news of her husband's illness impede her performance. Though uncertain of what a call with him would feel like—and where it may or may not lead—she focused on her budding romance with Kerry-Ann. Ashley let herself get carried away in self-expression of sensuality and love and tease throughout the show. She allowed herself the freedom to explore and to accept that the possibility of Kerry-Ann's position in her life was the answer to her loneliness. That, perhaps, Kerry-Ann was the love she was dreaming of—not a new man. Ashley tried not to overthink things. She moved fluidly, kept an open mind and receptive heart, and though it may have been an uncertain beginning, it was a new beginning no less, and she was ready to move forward.

Kerry-Ann was overwhelmed with pride—ecstatic and running on adrenaline when the cast and crew approached the stage for their final bow of the *Corsets and Cognac* showcase. Her only regret was that her father had not been there to see it live, but she made sure to send him videos that captured the moment. She was elated. And in need of a few days off to regroup. Kerry-Ann held a celebratory dinner with the cast and crew after closing, to mark what a beautiful journey they'd been on together. Felix had even unbothered during their meal despite Ashley and Kerry-Ann being seated next to each other. Maybe it was all in Kerry-Ann's head.

Together, the women were excited about what came next. Kerry-Ann couldn't wait to see how her next idea would materialize. Ashley wasn't sure if she had the energy to do another run but didn't know what else she'd do with all of the time that would now be freed up on her calendar. On the other hand, she liked the thought of only dating Kerry-Ann rather than dating *and* working together. She looked over her old journal entries and vision boards and came across several alternatives to burlesque. She didn't force herself to make any decisions, but instead opted to bask in the newness of her love life. After talking things over with Kerry-Ann and her son once more, she decided to give her ex-husband, Nathan, a call.

"Hello? Hello is anyone there?" he spoke into the phone several times. She shook and froze at the sound of his voice.

"Nathan, it's Ashley..." the three words were all she could muster. She was met with silence. An eerie silence.

"I swear to God, that boy doesn't listen," he huffed. "Ashley. Thanks for calling," he spoke as if the words pained him.

The call was brief. They went over what David already told Ashley. Though Nathan's reception was cold, Ashley felt there was a part of him that was grateful for the outreach. She let him know that she was willing to help with anything he needed. That she still cared for him.

"Well, thanks. Thank you..." he stuttered. "I'm fine now, but I do appreciate your sentiment. I do."

"Okay."

"I better get going, Ashley. Talk to you another time."

They said goodbyes. Pangs of guilt rocked her in the moments after she hung up. Would Nathan die sick and alone because of her? She pushed the thoughts out of her head, knowing there was no sense in antagonizing herself and reigniting old guilt over something that had already been resolved.

Ashley didn't know what she might be called upon to do, but she would take things as they come. As for right now, she wanted only to wade more deeply into a romance with Kerry-Ann and nurture her new love. And she wanted to mend her relationship with her son.

END

WHISKEY DUNGEON

CHAPTER 1

FRUSTRATION.

It bubbled up in me like slow-boiling water. It seems so obvious now how many opportunities I'd had over the last two decades to live life on my terms, but somehow the years slipped away in a white haze of doing what I thought would make me more influential. More successful. More . . . loveable. I'm full of regret, and I'm angry now. Sad even. I'd been too careless with time and too fearful of appearing imperfect to notice the loss that I bought into by selling myself short.

It's too bad it took losing my mother to a raw cocktail of health problems at 71 years old to realize my priorities were fucked up. Money. That's what I'd been focused on for too long. Status. That's what I constantly tried to build and reinforce. Power. That's what I ultimately wanted the most. But instead, I got anxiety, disappointment, self-pity, and lost moments I can never reclaim.

"Once again, everyone, welcome aboard Delta Flight 269 to Atlanta. Please be sure all large bags are stowed in an overhead bin." The flight attendant's announcements broke my introspection like an axe through a vintage wine barrel.

I'd been trying to pull myself together for seven months. I tried time off from work. Therapy. Vacations. Going back to church—everything. But each attempt was only a temporary fix. I still feel a hollowness inside. An unsteadiness. I don't want to build an empire anymore, but I don't know who I am without a career goal to pursue. I don't know what to do without a task list. I know this may sound crazy to many, but it's tragically real for me. I don't know what to feel without a constant source of drive to "climb the ladder." It feels like life tossed me into a strange land. An open land. And I must reinvent myself without rules or predetermined milestones of success.

"If you're seated in an exit row, please review the emergency exit seating criteria," the flight attendant droned on in the background, reminding me that I was returning home.

It had been a nightmare of a business trip, and I just wanted to get back already. I needed to figure out my next move.

I FELL asleep in my pod right after takeoff and woke up only for food and cocktails. The flight time went by relatively fast, and we were soon touching down in Atlanta. Thank God. If I didn't visit London again for a while, I wouldn't be upset about it. This is the second time a business deal fell through there, but this time it hurts more. This deal was bigger—multimillions in real estate—and it was supposed to be my gateway to a longer sabbatical, or even an early retirement. But things fell apart on a stupid administrative detail, which sparked a chain reaction of withdrawals from other investors that ultimately killed the entire plan. I couldn't get off the plane fast enough.

MORGAN L. CARTER. Seeing my name held up by a chauffeur always lifted my spirits a little. It was a sign of someone being there to help me for a change. I needed more of that.

"Good afternoon, Ms. Carter," he greeted me with a smile. "My name is Aiden, and I'll be taking you to your next stop."

I relaxed. "Hi, Aiden. Thank you so much."

Without any extra small talk, we made our way to baggage claim to grab my belongings before heading to my midtown condo. I was grateful for the professionalism and silence. In fact, I get overly excited when I get a driver who isn't chatty.

Traffic was unusually light for late afternoon in Atlanta, and we got to my building in record time. Another small win. Aiden helped me to the door with my things before whizzing off to his next job.

"Hey, Tanya." I forced a smile at my building receptionist. She was nice, but her baby hair and orange nails irritated my soul. Petty. I know. Shallow. I know. I'm working on it. I can be a judgmental asshole myself. Hell, maybe I shouldn't have quit therapy.

"I have a couple of packages for you." Tanya, unlike me, seemed to be in a good mood at work. She retrieved UPS and DHL parcels and handed them over the marble counter to me.

"Thank you." I softened. She didn't deserve my nasty attitude.

I'm not sure when my personality became critical, but I suspect it was gradual and in tandem with my pursuit of perfection. Growing up, I always felt like I deserved better. That I *was* better, smarter than most people, and deserving of a great life. I didn't have a particular reason. I just felt it in the core of my being, so I worked hard to achieve it. I wanted to be like Vanessa Williams, but with natural hair. Her grace, her poise, her elegance and the air of perfection that she gave off entranced me, so I studied her. I also studied bankers, business owners and other movers and shakers who started with nothing and worked their way to the top. I wanted the perfect life. Once I got it, I realized maintaining it was a nightmare, and now, I want out.

CHAPTER 2

I needed a drink. A stiff one. *Mmph. That's not the only stiff thing you need in your life.* Rude! Uninvited thoughts slinked across my mind before I could stop them, leaving an annoying revelation in their wake. I also needed to get laid. Anyone would at this point. It's been months, but it honestly feels like 525,600 minutes. But I was holding out. I'd promised myself that I would only share my body with partners whom I truly wanted to be in intimate space with. Not another guilty indulgence on a lonely night only to wake up regretful and still needing a proper orgasm. Until I met a man or woman who stirred my soul, I would please myself. The healing I needed wasn't in trysts—that much I knew was true. It was in finding what made me happy without outside influences and opinions.

So many conflicting thoughts ricocheted through my mind as I made an Old Fashioned on the rocks. Supposedly, it was "too early" for this kind of drink, but I was clawing my way out of social obligations to live a certain way. Wasn't it ridiculous to let random rules tell me what was acceptable and not acceptable in my own home, even when no one was looking? I wanted something other than a mimosa and gave myself permission to enjoy it. Baby steps.

It was Saturday morning and sunny. My condo was spotless,

which should have been a signal for me to relax and enjoy the day—I had a nerdy adventure planned for the evening—but instead, I was obsessing again. I wondered how I could feel so empty in a home full of reminders that my life was a dream to others.

A digital photo frame cycled through images of my girlfriends and me living it up in the city. Framed degrees recapped my education, from Florida A&M University to Georgia Institute of Technology —business administration and urban planning. I'd nailed both programs and earned my master's before zeroing in on real estate as a career. And up until recently, I loved my job.

I thrived on the challenge and beauty of commercial real estate. I enjoyed the powerful rooms it put me in as I reached greater heights. But somewhere along the way, I stopped finding happiness in business travel. I no longer cared for the accolades that came with "winning." Being booked and busy wasn't impressive to me anymore. It was exhausting and annoying.

There was always somewhere to be, but not *be* because of the social obligation to appear perfect and happy. I could never be myself —whoever that was—in most rooms. I had to be the picture of success. From my designer heels to my perfectly manicured nails and styled hair. Perfection. All the time. Then, there was always an email to answer, a notification to check, a person to meet, or a strained conversation with someone as interesting as a mosquito in my ear.

Even my downtime began to nosedive. I loved my friends, but I grew tired of brunches and endless Instagram Reels. I needed fresh excitement and wonder. Liberation from a life that felt plastic, formulaic even. I yearned for more meaningful moments, honesty, and intellectual conversations. I wanted to know what it felt like to *feel* everything—if that makes sense—instead of avoiding everything that didn't feed a perfect social perception. I sipped and pondered before cracking open my journal.

What can you be excited about today? That was the prompt of the day. *Easy*, I thought. I was doing something "out there." Seriously. I had plans to drive to the darkest part of Georgia to explore a childhood fascination of mine: astronomy. I'd almost forgotten about it until my therapist quizzed me on things that excited me before I knew what a career was. The memory was hidden in the recesses of my mind but resurfaced while I sat in front of him.

"Look at that," he'd said with a grin.

"What?" I'd felt self-conscious about mentioning something so far off from what I'd become.

"Your eyes," my therapist specified. "They glimmered when you said, 'Looking at the stars.' And I think I saw a mini smile trying to form on the left side of your mouth, but you suppressed it."

"Come on, Lucas." I was embarrassed.

He remained quiet, leaving me with my thoughts for several seconds before finally encouraging me to "explore it."

My leg shook and my hands tensed at his suggestion. It was a surprising memory that felt so left field and childish, but I promised I would do as he suggested. It took me months, though. After that session, I'd told Lucas I needed a break from everything—that my life was full, and I wasn't sure therapy was for me. I quit.

The truth is I wasn't accustomed to looking inside myself for answers, and I was uncomfortable with the process. Now, as I day drink, I realize that is what I *needed* to do to fix my life. He was right, so I started with that random youthful interest: stargazing.

It wasn't just the stars I liked; it was darkness itself—how endless, all-encompassing, grand, and expansive it was. The night sky was a black ocean I wished I could teleport into when I was a kid, I wrote in my journal. *My early childhood was filled with so many scary phrases about darkness that they planted seeds of curiosity about it in me. Figuratively and literally, because of religion.* I took another sip of my drink, deciding not to add much about religion to my journal entry. I didn't want to explore that just yet either. I wanted to focus on the potential fun ahead.

I was excited about honoring a voice I'd silenced for so long I didn't know if it still had strength to speak: my inner child. I wrote it all down. So many feelings ran amok inside me.

I was also nervous about driving two hours outside the city to meet random people in the dead of night. I was curious about what I might learn. I felt silly for going through with considering this a legitimate option for healing. Lots of emotions. I felt so ridiculous that I didn't tell anyone my plans, not even my daughter. Talk about role reversals—I never thought I'd need to hide anything I did from her, especially not something as dorky as stargazing, but fear overshadowed me. I put my pen down. That was enough journaling for today.

"THIS IS A CRAZY IDEA," I mumbled as I drove to the-middle-of-nowhere-Georgia later that evening. It was actually my second time —I'd tried it one morning so I could familiarize myself with the route during the day and met one of the regulars who told me the best evening to come back. This trip was different, though. The sun was still out, but I had an hour before it would begin setting. My palms sweat as I eased into the abandoned-looking town of Sharon, GA. Crumbling remnants of commerce abounded, and the "Welcome to Sharon" sign was written by hand. *What are you doing?* my inner critic interrogated, but I silenced her.

Trees grew inside of forgotten shops with concrete slabs, colorful doors, and brick walls but no roofs. "Yeah, this might be a very dumb idea!" I whispered aloud, giving an inch to decrying thoughts.

Sharon was a sleepy town, except for one place: Deerlick Astronomy Village—where I'd planned to spend the night. I kept going until I reached a point where the pavement ended, and the final stretch was a few hundred yards off-road. It was dusty and gravely. Signs to minimize my car lights appeared just before I reached the gate. This could have been the beginning of a horror movie, or it might have been the start of an adventurous new chapter. I kept going and found that once I was inside, Deerlick was pulsating with life.

"You came back!" a lanky car-mechanic-looking fellow greeted me gleefully at the entrance. "Morgan, right?" He wore an olive-green fishing hat over a mop of long hair, a NASA hoodie, and threadbare jeans.

"Yep, good memory." I smiled. "Jeff, right?"

"Indeed!" A grin peeked from a bushy gray beard.

Jeff had a faint Southern accent. He'd said he'd grown up in southern Georgia but moved around the country in his 20s to discover what else was out there. Now in his late 50s, he'd settled back in the South. He looked like he'd lived a life chock-full of stories. A tatted right hand and a chipped front tooth. On my first visit, he was kind to me, taking his time to explain what I might see on a clear evening.

"I see you brought an RV this time!" he said when we got to the main area, and I pulled into my assigned numbered slot—a small camper was waiting for me.

"Wanted to make it a bit more comfortable. I found a company that drops them off and picks them up for you."

"Get out of here!"

"No lie. I was too afraid to drive one myself, but this is a game-changer," I added.

"Well, I hope it gets the job done." Jeff held my gaze while not missing a beat setting up his gear. I tend to have that effect on people.

It was massive and a bit overwhelming to see the sky without obstruction as the sun began its descent. There were at least two dozen other vehicles parked around the village. Some people huddled in a warming tent to commune and beat the early evening chill. Others set up huge telescopes and camera rigging systems. It was a nerdy, friendly bunch.

As I got settled in, Riley—a chunky brunette with almond eyes and a country drawl—soon came over. She looked more like a farm girl than an amateur astronomer, and I wondered what led her to Deerlick. She probably wondered the same about me but didn't ask. I stood out as an obvious city girl with fitted camo pants, boyfriend-style sweater, and Wellington boots, but no one made a big deal of it outside of a few compliments. There was nothing more captivating than the sky that night, and I was fine with not being the center of attention for once.

Jeff, Riley, and I carried on, steadily preparing for our night under the cosmos, engaging in deep conversations that reflected the grandeur of our surroundings. Their chatter eventually faded into the background as I quietly wrestled with my thoughts.

The first time I'd visited, I was awash in thoughts of how minuscule our world was; how we—flimsy pockets of blood and bone—arrogantly ambled on our unkempt marble in a corner of a dark galaxy. While day turned to dusk, I still wondered about my place in the universe as the trees directed my gaze toward the enormous open sky. I fell into a meditation on ego and how we let it run rampant instead of centering our lives in love and community. We're barely aware of our consciousness yet fight, pillage, and argue about superiority among ourselves while being tiny flecks of life on a massive canvas. Why was mankind so ignorant and petty? I asked that question more times than I wanted to admit. Tonight, I hoped my contemplations would be more optimistic.

To make sure I made it through the night, I decided on a power nap after my initial mingle and setting up my gear. Thirty minutes later, the rattle of my cell phone jolted me out of sleep. It was my daughter. I exhaled, bracing myself for whatever financial request she was calling for this time. It's always a text until she needs money.

I swiped up to answer her video call. "Hey, Simone."

"Hey, Mom!" She looked beyond me. "Where are you?"

"In an RV. What's up?"

"In a what? Why? Are you *camping* or something?" Simone giggled. She was dumbfounded, not yet knowing the scope of the new me.

"Not camping in the traditional sense." I told her about my plans.

"You went to a random, cotton-picking town in southern Georgia by yourself?" Simone asked as though she were *my* parent.

Her concern amused me. "I did. You can relax, though. The last thing I'm threatened by is a bunch of astronomy geeks. I'm with good people in a beautiful space," I assured her. "It's just different. Now, what do you need?"

Simone took a gap year after high school and was on a four-week veterinary internship in Antigua, Guatemala. I wished I'd had the same opportunity when I was her age. Well, I did, but gap years weren't a thing back then, and there's no way my parents would've signed off on me going to another country alone for a month. I tried to give my daughter more freedom, trusting that her father and I equipped her to survive mostly on her own.

"Who said I needed something?" Simone asked incredulously. "I love your hair, by the way."

"You don't?" Sometimes I still couldn't believe I had a 19-year-old. "And thank you. I missed having crochet locs."

"I do want help! But you didn't have to assume that from the jump," she laughed. "I don't need a lot. It's just—I can tell I might run out of money because I keep spending it on supplies for some of the kids I meet."

"Remember what I told you about not standing out too much. You can help, but I don't want you to look like an ATM."

"I don't. I promise."

"I mean it. It's about safety."

"I know, Mom! Plus . . . I want to take a weekend trip to Costa Rica, if that's okay with you."

"Ah ha. There it is!" We laughed simultaneously. What a life! "How much?"

"Just enough for the plane ticket. I did some freelance work online and should have my money from that in a few days. That'll take care of my pocket money. I just need you to help me get there, please." She batted her eyelashes and flashed a big, goofy grin.

It's hard to say no when you're face-to-face. "Okay," I gave in. I didn't have a real reason to say no. Simone was a great kid. Hard-working, never in trouble, charming with a gift for wielding her personal power—I wanted to raise her differently than my mean and tight-fisted parents raised me.

"Can you Zelle me?" She asked. "I might get a cheaper flight if I book it myself from here."

"Of course."

"Thank you! I love you so much, Mom!"

"You're welcome." I wanted to add, "Next time, ask your father" but held myself back.

Simone's dad and I had come a long way since our 20s. He'd always been a good father despite his initially wanting me to get an abortion. I refused, and we split at the seams as a couple, squabbling and disagreeing over everything for the sake of contention. Neither of us wanted to give an inch to the other in Simone's early years. I figured he never wanted her in the first place, so why should he tell me how to raise her? He argued that he wasn't ready to be a dad but that since I forced him into it, he should have a say in her activities. We hated each other, but he did always pay his child support, and in time, we both matured. In fact, he sent more than he was required to. Andre just didn't want to start a family so young, especially with *me*.

I was a wildly different person when I had Simone. Looking back, I wouldn't have wanted to marry me either if I were him. He was too free-spirited to consent to cultural traditions that commanded marriage just because a child was born. I didn't understand and took it deeply personally then, but I know better now. Now. . .all I want is freedom. I crave a place to feel safe to explore my passions. I want to feel alive.

A tap on my window pulled me back into the present moment. It was Jeff.

"Hi!"

"Say, Morgan, I wanted to show you something since you were asking about how I got such clarity in my photos last time." A flash of apologetic concern crossed his face. "I'm sorry. I should have waited until you came back out. Pardon my intrusion. I just got excited about showing you something," Jeff rambled.

"It's fine. Don't worry about it. I was just about to make some hot chocolate. Would you like some?"

"That sounds great," Jeff smiled. "I'd love some, thanks!"

"No problem. What's up?"

"I remember you saying you were originally from Philly and never got to see much like this because of all the light pollution."

"I did. Great memory." I was impressed by his attention to detail in conversation. It was rare to find that in a man, in my experience.

Jeff patiently explained technical aspects of his set-up and showed me how I could get the best images using the gear that I'd brought. "Whatever you have is enough. I promise you just have to know how to use what you already have to get what you want. It's enough."

Not long after, we sank into the glory of the night. Reflective. Inspired. Entranced. I was giddy with excitement yet contemplative. The evening was perfect.

I WOKE up with a crick in my neck. Sleeping in the RV was a hell of a lot better than my Tesla, but somehow, I managed to lie in an awkward position for most of the night that left me feeling like a tin man in the morning. The sunrise drew me out of sleep despite having rested for only four hours. Even with the curtains drawn, the sun blazed through. I wasn't ready to head back to Atlanta just yet and spent the morning cooking one of my favorite breakfast concoctions —protein-packed pancakes topped with gooey cheddar cheese, green apple slices, real maple syrup, and bacon, along with a heaping of scrambled eggs. I'd had the overindulgence once in Montreal and never forgot it. I battled feeling guilty for not going for a run after, which is what I'd normally do to make sure I stayed in shape. I was learning to say no to what I thought I was supposed to do and yes to what I *wanted* to do. I wanted a life that fed my pleasure zones without shame. That's a hard goal to keep from day to day. It went against almost everything I was trained and had reinforced myself to do for decades.

The mix of my religious upbringing and societal ideals once imprisoned me in a state of constant misery. "Don't eat this. Don't do that. Don't think this. You shouldn't feel that. Don't enjoy these foods. Don't fantasize about sex. Don't embrace your body the way it is. You are sinful and imperfect, so buy this to fix it or pray to change that." I was crippled from all the constraints, but inch by inch, I chipped away at the confinement of my mind and life of the limited beliefs I'd had. All I wanted was freedom. And passion. I wanted it in everything I did, regardless of the cost.

CHAPTER 3

I hate people who wear Crocs; they look like assholes. *Be nice.* My inner voice reminded me to restrain my urge to judge others' appearance as I walked into a time-worn gas station. The bell above the door jingled when I stepped inside, announcing my presence.

"Welcome!" A weary cashier looked up from her coffee, offering a wrinkled, closed-mouth smile and nod with her greeting.

"Hello." I smiled and scanned the place.

I didn't even need gas; I needed water, but from the looks of it, everything inside might've been dusty and expired. The air carried a musty scent of stale coffee and forgotten dreams.

There was hardly a trace of patronage, save for a lone trucker engrossed in a map and a guy wearing a T-shirt from a '90s sitcom, black hoochie daddy shorts, and a pair of canary-colored Crocs—a fashion disaster of comfort screaming over style.

"Let me know if I can help you find anything," the cashier piped up.

"Just looking for water, thanks."

"Last aisle on the right. Bottom shelf. The refrigerator's broken, so none of 'em are cold, sorry," she said.

"That's fine." I immediately walked to the back to get what I needed so I could leave. It was at this moment I found myself shoulder to shoulder with Mr. Crocs.

I glanced to my side, taking in the banana footwear that had caught my attention earlier. Mr. Crocs stood there, a quirky yet confident smile sweeping his face when he noticed me. Our unexpected proximity created a brief pause in my rush to leave and sparked a curiosity that I couldn't ignore. *Who raised him?* I wanted to laugh but I didn't. I wanted to look him up and down once more, but I held back. Instead, I reached for the last bottle of water—unwittingly and simultaneously as he did, our fingers grazing each other's. *Fuck. Now, I* have to *speak to him.* We exchanged a glance before breaking into a smile, recognizing the serendipity of the moment.

"Looks like we have a classic bottle standoff here," he said, his voice laced with playful humor.

What a cornball, I thought. "Is that so?" I didn't know how else to respond.

"Yup. So, how about we strike a compromise? Let's split the water. Sharing is caring, right?"

I was speechless and dumbfounded.

He grinned. "My name is Caleb," he said, extending his hand, "and of course, I'm kidding."

"Morgan." I gave in. He had a beautiful smile, I had to admit. I decided to play along in effort to relax and be more in the moment. It was one of my personal goals. "So, how do you suppose we split this?"

Caleb lit up. "Well, you're in luck because I happen to be an expert when it comes to water sharing and women. And you must be the goddess who's about to make my day more refreshing."

I couldn't help but laugh at his confidently goofy introduction.

"There it is. A smile. A beautiful one, at that," he complimented. "We can get out of here if you want. I'll pay for the water if you at least let me know if I might ever see you again." He quickly added to his statement before I could respond. "I *know* you can buy your own water, Morgan. Humor me."

I rubbed my forehead. I should have driven past this grubby gas station.

Caleb began walking to the counter without getting my answer, but he stopped abruptly and spun around. "Wait a minute," he said, his voice tinged with excitement. "Were you at Deerlick last night?"

My eyes widened, and I halted my step. "Yes, I was. Were you there too?"

"Indeed, I was." He continued walking to the cashier, reworking his trivial banter to thoughtful appreciation as he addressed her. "Ma'am, I'm so glad I popped into your store today!"

"So am I!" She smiled. "It's pretty slow around here, if you couldn't tell." She chuckled lightly, revealing a gapped-tooth grin.

Caleb didn't miss a beat. "You know, your smile has the power to turn a mundane errand into a fateful encounter." He leaned on the counter, I assumed flashing his mischievous smile at her.

Nice butt, I thought. *Legs too.* Despite his gaudy shoes, Caleb clearly did care about his physique. It wasn't until this moment that I fully looked him over, noticing the broadness of his back and shoulders. He was short, with glasses and remnants of what was probably the body of a god. I walked closer and stood by his side instead of behind him, noticing a gray patch in his bushy beard. A closer look at his arms revealed a fine layer of hair on his skin, adding to the texture of his toffee-colored complexion. The hair on his head was soft, coily with a touch of gray on the temples.

"My friend here needs some water, and it looks like this was the last bottle. Do you happen to have any cases in the back?"

"Unfortunately, that's all I've got until a new delivery comes in. Sorry, honey," she said.

"It's all good." He slapped a $20 bill on the counter.

This guy still carries cash, I noted.

"By the way, we were both at Deerlick last night," Caleb kept chatting. "Small world, huh?"

The cashier's eyebrows shot up in surprise. "No kidding! Well, consider it a cosmic coincidence. I'll ring up that water for you, and I'll give you one from my personal stash. How's that?"

"That's perfect!"

As the cashier scanned the bottle, Caleb turned to me with a grin. "So, Morgan, promise to let me know if I'll ever see you again?"

"Say yes, honey. Just see what happens," the cashier encouraged.

I exhaled and, as if to answer them both at once, I gave in. "Sure."

With a playful wink, Caleb paid for the waters, thanked the shopkeeper, and led the way outside. I followed him.

Caleb drove a sand-colored Polestar—the only other car that could possibly be his was parked just a space over from mine. "Nice car," I commented, curious about his choice.

Caleb beamed. "Thanks! I'm all about the intersection of style and sustainability."

"And mystery too?"

"Huh?" He handed me one of the waters he'd been holding.

"Why would anyone choose that over a Tesla?" I teased. "The latter is obviously the better decision."

"Only if you like going with the crowd, Morgan. I'm a man of my own lane. My own way. My own actions." Caleb looked me directly in the eyes without blinking. "Plus, this car embodies my personality."

"Dynamic and fearless, clearly," I responded.

"I try." He turned his body away from me. "Look, it's been great running into you here. I do hope to hear back from you. Even if it's just for lunch. I'm just outside of Atlanta, how about you?"

"Midtown. In the city."

"Call me. That's all you have to do, and I'll take care of the rest." He reached into his pocket for his phone and pulled up an app with his contact info. "Scan this, and everything will show up for you."

This guy was definitely different, and I found myself growing more intrigued by the minute. I went ahead and took his information, already knowing I'd call later.

"I'll see you around, Morgan. I can't wait to hear about your experience at Deerlick and what brought you out here."

I smiled and, before I could speak, Caleb began walking to the driver's side door of his car. And just like that, he drove off.

CHAPTER 4

Caleb Whittaker. I glanced at the contact card that saved to my phone from his QR code. What an interesting character to drop into my life. As much as I wanted to pretend I didn't care about his walking away without looking back, I really did. He had a cocky assurance that I wasn't used to—one I wasn't sure I wanted to play right into by calling him. But he had a magnetic pull that I felt long after I got home.

I resisted the urge for the evening—it had been a long day, and I still needed to process my evening under the stars—but I knew I'd call him by the following afternoon. The way he casually said, "I'm a man of my own lane. My own way. My own actions" stuck with me. His confidence, though bordering on arrogance, fascinated me. Was it genuine or just a facade?

~

As I settled into my condo, my mind wandered to dinner. I'm not fond of cooking and paid for the convenience of weekly chef-prepared meals to make sure I made the healthiest choices. It would be seared snapper with quinoa and roasted vegetables tonight, I decided—with a glass of white wine. My condo was quiet, and as I ate, I happened to glance up at a digital photo frame across the room and caught a glimpse of my mom and myself. She was so beautiful before illness destroyed her. So smart. So nurturing and kind. We didn't always see eye to eye because of her unwavering Christianity and attempt to preach the gospel every time we spoke, but in her final year, she stopped pushing. I don't know if her faith began to crack or if she finally realized that I wouldn't go back down that road. Maybe it was a bit of both.

"I miss you, Mom." The words slipped out of my mouth with ease.

Religion also ravaged my relationship with my daughter's father and a string of partners after him. I thought it was them when each connection crashed and burned, but by my third lover, I realized the problem might be me. It was me who had felt guilty or ashamed of everything that gave me pleasure. It was me who hid and avoided my innate desires for so long that I forgot what they were. It was me who constantly worried and overthought that people might find out about my secret desires. I was the problem, and therapy revealed that. It also helped me realize it wasn't too late to explore all the things my younger self craved.

My night at Deerlick showed me the benefits of saying yes to scary things. Not that stargazing itself was frightening, but walking into a decades-old fascination despite feeling foolish was expansive. It gave me the opportunity to conquer a part of myself and connect with new people. From Jeff and Riley to Caleb—each of them offered a new path to unique experiences and different kinds of conversations and connection—more depth, less surface, because they were out indulging their passions versus mindlessly going to more socially expected activities like Dîner en Blanc and red-carpet events. I had a great time and opened more doors to authentic connections. I wanted more of that!

As the night wore on, I daydreamed about other activities I'd always wanted to try. Snorkeling. Scuba diving. Skiing. They all involved the outdoors. I loved nature, and the more I thought about it, the more I realized the irony of my career being all about transactions and selling commercial spaces. I was overdue to step outside those walls and explore the untamed world, where nature and passions intertwine. Speaking of passion, I also found myself aroused, but alone. My hormones were raging again. This time, I gave in—opting for a warm shower with the intention to love on myself like I hadn't in a long time.

It was all sensual for me. The pace of my breathing, feeling the water on my skin and the texture of my loofah sponge as I slowly ran it against my body. I took big inhales and exhales, giving myself the presence to notice everything from the temperature and steam to the pressure of the water. I slowed down enough to notice how soapsuds slid down my skin. Being more intentional and present with myself was another goal of mine. I only hoped someone else would be thoughtful enough to do the same for me one day.

I calmed my hormones down by focusing on nonsexual sensation and sensory pleasure. By the time I crawled into bed, though, I allowed them to rev back up enough for me to enjoy myself with one of my favorite sex toys: the rose. The only problem was—which I realized the next morning when I woke up—that I was so relaxed that I fell asleep before reaching any kind of firework ending! The toy lay next to me, almost out of battery from flicking its electric tongue at nothing all night. *That's a damn shame*, I thought, laughing at myself.

Caleb was still on my mind, but I didn't want to call him too early, so I delayed until midmorning. Then he answered on the second ring.

"This is Caleb—the one *everyone* is talking about." I could tell he was smiling through his voice.

"Umm . . ." His greeting caught me so off guard that I didn't know what to say.

He remained devilishly silent.

"Caleb. Hey, it's Morgan." I finally found my words.

"Morgan!" He seemed genuinely surprised. "I was just playing around. I usually don't answer calls from unknown numbers."

"But you did today. Hmm. . .Maybe something's up with the stars."

"In the daytime?"

"They're always there, even if we don't see them," I told him.

"Touché."

"Did I catch you at a good time?"

"Not really, but I'll make it the right time. Can you give me a sec?"

"Sure." I was already grinning. I wondered what I'd interrupted, what he did for a living, where he lived. I was shockingly curious about him.

"Hey there, I'm back. I'm really glad you called; you know?"

"Did you think I wouldn't?"

"You can never be too sure, but I was hopeful."

"Well, here I am. I was hoping it wasn't too early—figured you'd just send it to voice mail if you were busy. But . . . I'll admit you captured my intrigue, and I'm too old to play telephone waiting games when I sense chemistry with someone. Anyway, I didn't catch what you did for a living."

"I appreciate that. And I do several things for a living! The main one is farming. I own a big one. I'm also a YouTuber and a personal chef."

"Wow!"

"You mean you didn't see any of that coming?"

"No, Caleb. Not at all." *A farmer/YouTuber/chef?!* This guy was full of surprises!

"Third-generation farmer, actually. I don't do much in the fields these days, although I know how to. It's more like managing any other business. Hard work. Lots of risks. Knowing how to assess markets and finding ways to diversify my products. How about you?" Caleb pinged me before I could soak up his words.

"Commercial real estate sales." I suddenly felt self-conscious.

"Do you love it?"

"I used to." I felt my body slump after answering.

"Interesting choice, commercial real estate sales. Are you the type to wine and dine clients at fancy restaurants, or do you prefer sealing deals while attending exclusive charity events?" Caleb quizzed.

"Both, actually. Do you have any fancy restaurant recommendations?" I tried to keep pace with his banter, grateful that he didn't ask why I don't love real estate anymore.

"I do. Maybe I'll share them with you after we get to know each other a little better. I can't give you all my secret pleasures right away, you know?" He chuckled.

I liked him and couldn't wipe the smile off my face. "Fair enough. So, let's say I want to get to know you better. What's the best way to go about doing that? What are your interests? What brought you to Deerlick? And why in God's name were you wearing those yellow Crocs?"

"Don't hate! Those shoes are the bomb. I wore them because *I* like the comfort they provide, and I was feeling sunny yesterday."

"You sure have a way with words!"

"I have a way with everything, darling," he teased. "And to answer your question, I went out there to find peace. I'm not much of an astronomy person or science nerd, but I'd heard about it online and figured, why not? It seemed fun enough."

"How'd you like it?"

"Fascinating. That big sky really puts things—and us—in perspective if you let it. It's beautiful and humbling to observe. What about you? What brought you from Midtown, Atlanta, to bumfuck, Georgia? Are you really a country girl at heart, or . . ."

"Not really."

"Ah, so you're a city girl with a taste for adventure; I see. I like it. It adds to your allure. As for me, I was born and raised in Treutlen County—just two hours outside of the city. I'm a man of many experiences and interests, but my heart belongs to that land. The farm has been in my family for generations."

"It must be rewarding to carry on your family's legacy."

"It has its challenges, but I do my best." He stopped short of continuing. It felt abrupt.

I let the silence linger, not racing to fill it in. If there's anything that I'll always take with me from doing real estate deals, it's that whoever speaks first usually loses. Not that Caleb and I were negotiating, but I know there's power in my silence and not rushing to cover it with chatter.

"But that isn't the only thing that defines me," he finally continued.

"Is it being a chef or your YouTube personality? I want to see your channel, by the way."

"All of that and then some." He hesitated again. "Hey, look, Morgan. There's something else I want to share with you. I believe in honesty and being upfront, so I want you to know that I'm a transgender man."

My eyes bulged. *What did he say?*

"There's never an easy way to say that," he continued, "but I can already tell we have chemistry, and I want to give you the chance to decide if this changes anything for you. I know it's not something everyone's comfortable with."

Caleb felt like a freight train with no brakes. I appreciated his honesty and didn't know if I would've appreciated more time or if he did the right thing getting it out of the way early. I spoke softly, "Thank you for telling me. I appreciate your openness."

There was another silence. I'd never been told this before and didn't have a knee-jerk reaction either way. Caleb looked so . . . biologically male. I would have never guessed. I felt my left foot beginning to nervously tap as if an internal clock were pressing me to say something. I didn't know how to answer. I didn't know what to do. *A trans man?*

Fuck it. I heard myself beginning to speak. "Your identity doesn't change the connection we've established or the person who I was anxious to call, so . . ." I paused. "Yeah, let's keep getting to know each other. I'm open-minded."

He was upbeat. "Thank you. I appreciate your understanding and am really looking forward to learning more about you!"

"So, when is a good time to talk again? Earlier, you said this wasn't the best."

"Anytime after 3:00. I'll call you back this time. Sound good?"

"Absolutely."

"Great, talk to you soon!" Caleb said before we both ended the call.

My therapist would really be proud of me for leaning into the crazy and saying yes instead of running from it. I couldn't think of a more unexpected turn for me to take, but I was ready for wherever it was leading me. At least, I hoped so.

CHAPTER 5

To avoid overthinking until Caleb called back, I busied myself with work. Emails. Phone calls. Another cycle of "touching base" while killing time. Boring ass shit! As the time ticked on, I went through moments of caring and not caring about the outcomes of any of the deals I was working on. To make the moments of caring last long enough to do a good job, I had to grasp at the fading version of myself. The truth was I didn't care anymore. None of it mattered.

As the day wound down, I decided to make a more tangible list—with dates—of the activities I wanted to try and places I wanted to visit. That was much more exciting than cap rates, gross leases, and absorption rates—all the mundane jargon of commercial real estate.

I decided to start with snorkeling. It was March, and though warmer weather was making itself apparent, a Caribbean vacation sounded the most appealing at the moment. *Hmm . . . where should I go?* I wondered. *Mexico, The Bahamas, Honduras?* I looked around for inspiration on TikTok and even asked my AI chatbot to do a country-to-country comparison before I landed on The Bahamas. It was a shorter flight, had no language barriers, and held the unbeatable promise of Caribbean food! With a snorkeling excursion booked at The Bahamas' stunning Rose Island Reefs, I felt a sense of excitement begin building up in me again!

CALEB CALLED me back later that evening, just as he'd promised. "You have an intoxicating voice, you know that? Has anyone ever told you?" he asked.

"No," I blushed. "Not quite like that."

"It's like, umm . . ." He paused to collect his thoughts. "It's like a sip of the finest aged whiskey, especially the way you say my name. You make 'Caleb' sound like a warm, velvet pour," Caleb described, his voice filled with admiration.

"Wow. Well, thank you, Caleb. Are you a fan of poetry?" I had to ask based on his response.

"I am. I don't write it myself, but I follow a lot of lesser-known folks on social media. You?"

"I haven't read any in a while, but I recently started reading more fiction. It's a nice retreat from the real world."

"I've been getting that's a real need for you—escaping your reality. From stargazing and how you talked about your job. Are you just burnt out with your life, or . . ."

"Yes, but I'm actively changing it into what I want it to be."

"And what's that?"

"More authentic. More curious. More . . . passionate."

Caleb's voice dripped with amusement as he teased, "Oh, I see you're on a quest for the extraordinary, huh? Careful now; you might end up setting more than just your own soul ablaze."

I played along. "Well, some fires are worth spreading. Who knows —maybe I'll inspire others to do the same."

He chuckled, his voice brimming with charm. "I have no doubt about that. But remember, passion can be a double-edged sword. It can consume you if you're not careful."

"What do you mean by that?" I wanted to make sure I interpreted his statement correctly.

"Well, I'm all for passion—sometimes to depths and lengths beyond what most people are comfortable with—but I embraced it for long enough to know that unchecked or unbalanced passion can lead to obsession or neglecting other aspects of life. So, it's all about balance. Never let passion make you lose sight of boundaries or become overly fixated on one thing. At least, that's what I've learned so far."

"Insightful. Thank you for elaborating. I'm no stranger to playing with fire. I've danced with it, let it fuel my ambitions to the point of creating a career that's as indelible as the finest whiskey. But . . ." The more I spoke, the more I realized he was right.

"But what?"

"I guess . . ." It was hard for me to say the words out loud. "I guess you could say that lead me to where I am now." I laughed at myself.

"Unbalanced? Hungry for more? Searching?"

"Yeah. And then you showed up."

"Like a ray of sunshine!"

"Literally!" We shared a beautiful exchange, likely creating our first inside joke by playing on his shoes and his being like sunshine. "You are a breath of fresh air, I'll admit. I want to see you again," I confessed.

"So do I! Would you be interested in checking out a local art studio?"

"That sounds fun."

"Great! I'll do some research and find one close to you."

"Thank you!" It felt so good to have him be so immediately decisive. I loved it!

"You're quite welcome. Give me a day or two, and I'll have a few options for you. Sound good?"

"That sounds perfect." I smiled.

Caleb and I talked a bit longer about creativity, his farm, and his chef business—he promised that if we made it to a second date, he'd cook for me—and the hours slipped by effortlessly. Unspoken chemistry brewed between us. By the time we wound our conversation down, it felt as though we'd set a promising foundation for a fun, and maybe tantalizing, first date.

CHAPTER 6

Getting to know Caleb was exhilarating. He was definitely a different kind of man, and I was enamored with him quicker than I thought possible. He chose an interactive art studio for our first date where we not only learned about sculpting but got our hands dirty creating a sculpted pair of ceramic lips. It was artistic, playful, alluring and almost seductive doing it together.

We talked a lot over the next two weeks. He told me that he wasn't actively looking for a serious girlfriend, and that he didn't want to commit to one person but would always be honest about his health status and anything else that would be important to me if we began to see each other seriously. Caleb was a lot. He was more honest than any person I'd ever been with. He was surer of himself, but also seemed to crave connection, especially from someone who could be fluid and fun.

As much as he excited me, he also made me nervous. I'd always looked at dating and relationships as having to "go somewhere." Caleb's admission of his needs challenged the lens through which I looked at dating. *It's not a waste of time if you're enjoying yourself and not hell bent on a final destination*, he'd said during one of our talks. *I don't like pressure,* he'd added. *But I do like the joyride of getting to know new people and am particular about who I share my body with, so you don't have to worry about me being irresponsible in that way.* I was afraid of the unknown in dealing with him, but I couldn't stop myself from wanting more interactions. We spent time at a covert speakeasy and just before my trip to the Bahamas, Caleb invited me to a local restaurant where he'd struck some kind of deal with the owner to cook and serve me dinner in a private room.

"Now, I've noticed we both have a thing for whiskey," he'd said when he went over menu options to make sure I didn't have any dietary restrictions.

"That is correct."

"Perfect. With that in mind, I created a menu that I hope will trigger every tastebud in your mouth and have you begging for more."

"I'm ready!" I laughed.

"First up are Whiskey-Glazed Bacon-Wrapped Dates," he announced, "they're brushed in a brown sugar and cayenne pepper sauce made from one of my favorite bottles."

Holy fuck. They tasted amazing. "These are delicious, Caleb!"

He smiled proudly as he took a bite of his own. "Chef kiss!" He proclaimed before blitzing back to the kitchen. He left me with a small Bluetooth speaker streaming a playlist he'd curated for our date. The sounds were relaxing, almost like you'd expect in a spa. When he came back, he brought two salad plates and sat down with me.

"I got some help back there, so a waiter will bring out the main dish and dessert."

"How do I know you aren't cheating and your 'help,'" I spoke teasingly, "isn't the one doing all the cooking?"

"Oh, I can guarantee you that! One day, if you'll allow it, I'll invite you to my place so I can dazzle you real-time with no visual obstructions. I just thought doing it this way would make you more comfortable."

"You were correct. Thank you."

"So, are you excited about your trip? Have you been to the Bahamas before?"

"I am! And yes, but only as a stop on a cruise. This'll be my first time flying in directly."

"I'm thrilled for you, and hope you have a great time. I'm not a big fan of the water. I can't even swim, to be honest with you."

"I learned as a kid and did it here and there as an adult. I'm not a super swimmer or anything, but I am fascinated with the ocean."

"Just like the sky."

"Yes. They're both so much bigger than us that they pull me in."

Before he could respond, the waiter came to clear our empty plates and bring out the next dish.

"This," Caleb began explaining, "is Herb-Crusted Salmon with Whiskey Butter Sauce...speaking of the ocean. I hope you're not too fond of fish to eat them," he joked.

"No!" I grinned. "I love salmon."

"I know. I'm messing with you. I made sure to stick to info I phished out of you regarding your tastes in food the last few weeks."

"You little devil, you."

"I can be a bigger devil if you want," he looked into my eyes as without blinking. His words were flirtatious, but his stare was piercing.

"Maybe...maybe." I blushed.

Caleb's eyes widened a little – just enough for me to know that my response made him smile inside. "Noted."

WE CONTINUED TO EAT, talk and flirt all the way through his divine dessert – a grand finale of Vanilla Whiskey Creme Bruleé topped with fresh berries and a sparkling candle. Needless to say, this one of the best dates I'd ever been on. He was kind, witty, flirtatious and nerd-sexy. I loved his intellect and self-assuredness. There was a lot packed in his short stature. By the end of our meal, I'd inched closer to rest my hand on his leg. We were seated side by side rather than opposite each other like most restaurants would have sat us if our meal was with everyone else.

"Caleb, this was a beautiful experience," I admitted. "Thank you for your thoughtfulness, your planning and just ... everything. I really enjoyed this."

"You are so welcome! It's been a while since I've connected with anyone like this."

"As charming as you are?"

"Yes, even with my impeccable charm!" He laughed. "I don't go out as much as I used to. Work has kept me busy, and outside of that, I've spent a lot of time renovating a part of my house to make it more fun."

"How so?"

"Don't worry about all that – you're not ready." Caleb eased from under my touch and began clearing the table with a smile.

"Wait. What?"

He kept clearing with a smug smirk on his face and walked toward the kitchen.

"Caleb!" I demanded when he returned. "How are you just going to get up and not answer me like that?" I laughed. The audacity and mystery of this man.

"Because I can. And because I'm right. You're not ready."

"So why did you bring it up?"

"I don't know. But I get the feeling you're vanilla, so like I said, don't worry about it."

"Asshole."

"Oh, how we went from compliments and how wonderful I've been to me being an asshole!"

"I'm kidding. But I want to know what you mean! And what do you mean calling me vanilla?" Curiosity was killing me.

He sighed and sat back down. "I'm finishing up an adult playroom." He spoke without blinking.

Shit. Maybe he was right. Maybe I wasn't ready for the adventurous side he was hinting at. "Okay," I filled the empty air with the only word that came to mind. An adult playroom? The idea intrigued and intimidated me simultaneously.

Caleb's eyes searched mine, gauging my reaction. "Maybe I shouldn't have mentioned it," he said, his voice tinged with concern.

"No, no," I quickly responded, not wanting to discourage him. "I'm just... surprised, that's all. I never thought... well, I guess I never expected this."

He leaned forward, his expression gentle yet filled with anticipation. "Look, I understand if it's too much, or if it's not your thing. I was just being honest about my life. I would *never* push you into something you're not comfortable with, I promise you that."

My heart raced. Interest. Trepidation. Excitement. Reservation. A whirlwind of emotions funneled inside me. I felt my leg gently shaking in anxiety. This was a crossroads, an opportunity to explore a new side of myself. It was a chance to step out of my comfort zone and embrace another unknown. "It's fine," I finally said, meeting his gaze. "I...want...to know more." My words were measured.

A mixture of relief and excitement washed over Caleb's face. He reached over to gently take my hand in his. "I'm glad to hear that. If you can't tell already, I'm an open book."

His words resonated with me, and I nodded affirmatively.

"You can trust me, and I'm big on communication so, I also want you to always feel safe to express how you feel, okay?"

"Okay. Thank you." I felt comforted.

"Now...do you want to go for a walk before heading home? We can keep talking."

"That's a great idea, especially after eating all that food! It was delicious though."

Caleb beamed and outstretched his hand to help me up from my seat.

AS THE EVENING CONTINUED, our conversation shifted, grazing the surface of our desires, boundaries, and experiences. I shared that I hadn't experienced as much pleasure and passion as I thought I should have by this point in my life. I shared how my religious upbringing chained me to limited and scant views on what was acceptable and expected and enormous opinions on what was wrong and sinful—that though I've long since broken free, I'd never met anyone I'd felt safe enough...or even inspired enough to contemplate transcending the ordinary. Caleb held my hand firmly and shared a bit of his story. He'd never gone to church and had always been a bit of an outcast. He'd known before puberty that he identified as male and transitioned early – before his outward appearance could fully look like the gender he was assigned at birth. Being within the LGBTQIA community was a natural path for him to find himself in communities that encouraged a full exploration of himself.

"I've spent more time than most people discovering and under-standing who I am," he said. "I'm still learning. It's a lifelong thing, you know? I just think that it's easier for those of us who never fit into social norms because we *must* define ourselves for ourselves or be misunderstood."

I listened intently, absorbing his words with my entire being.

"Now, the adult play stuff came later in life," he laughed. "Just so we're clear. I don't want you thinking I knew all of that as a teenager. Years later, I met someone who became the spark to awaken me to a realm of previously unknown pleasure."

Caleb and I continued chatting as we rounded a corner back to where our cars were parked. I'd learned so much from him that night. He triggered something in me that made me more aware of myself as a sexual being, and that my sexuality wasn't in a vacuum or supposed to be compartmentalized. Any shame, bashfulness or guilt I held around it affected my ability to be open, fluid and free in other parts of my life.

"Sexual energy is deeply tied to creative expression, and creative expression is how you really unleash your true self," Caleb said when we reached the parking lot.

"Mr. Poetry – there you go again."

"It's a gift, I can't help it!" he smiled.

I stepped closer to him, ready to feel his body heat. He pulled me closer, not missing a beat and finally, we kissed. My body trembled with excitement, and I could feel my heart beating in my ears when his salt-and-pepper beard touched my skin. Our kiss went deep. He pulled me even closer, resting his hands at the small of my back. For a few moments, I was totally absorbed and quickly aroused. But that's when I felt a jolt snatching me out of the moment. We were outside kissing like teenagers and something in me felt embarrassed and self-conscious.

"What's wrong?" he asked.

"Nothing," I lied. I wasn't proud of my feelings.

Caleb caressed my back and placed a tiny space between us. "Tonight was fun."

"Yes, it was! I can't wait to do it again." I regained my composure.

"As soon as you get back from your trip?"

"Yeah...that works," I smiled.

He leaned in to kiss me on the cheek before bidding me good night. That was the end of the most interesting, stimulating and sensory-engaging first date I'd had in my entire life.

CHAPTER 7

"You ever dived with sharks before?"

"Uhh no." I'd barely ever dived at all.

"It's okay. It's not as scary as it sounds." The chummy tour guide comforted. His sweaty bronze skin glistened under the Bahamian morning sun.

"I thought we were snorkeling today?" Was I mistaken? I panicked.

"We are. Don't worry, mama. I was just curious," he clarified in his sing-song Caribbean accent.

A week after my rendezvous with Caleb, I was aboard a tour boat in glistening warm waters. I had never been beyond the shore of an ocean in such a tiny boat, and there I was on a ferry heading so far that land was a dot in the distance. I hoped there were no sharks out there. It seemed asinine to go into the natural habitat of another animal and hope it didn't show up, but whatever. There were a few enthusiasts aboard, so I wasn't alone. I was excited!

"Everybody alright?" Our guide quizzed.

The water got choppy the further out we went. It was rougher than he'd had anticipated, but he promised it would get smoother once we got to the site with the coral reef. My adrenaline pumped when we finally arrived. I felt a bit queasy.

"Want a ginger chew?" A fellow passenger offered. "It'll help settle your stomach."

I smiled but politely declined. I had a thing about accepting food from strangers. "I'm okay, thank you." I told her. "I can breathe through it."

Breathe. I'd learned that was the key to almost everything—controlling your breath, that is. If there was one thing I'd mastered so far on my personal journey it was the power of breath control and knowing how much it could impact my well-being. I took a few moments to center myself on the boat while most others had jumped off to explore. Inhale. Exhale. Slowly. Again...I inhaled deeply, held it for five seconds, and then exhaled. I repeated one more time before grabbing my gear and joining the others.

The water was still turbulent when we jumped in. It was warm and swallowed me like an eager lover – *maybe the way Caleb would*, I thought, shocking myself. Memories of our dates flooded me as I swam to the spots where everyone pooled together. I thought of him as I went under, taking in the different species of fish and stunning underwater scenery. There was so much life teaming around me that I quickly fell in love, captivated by every little colorful creature that swam by.

The last time I'd done something like this was on a cruise with my daughter's dad decades before. It was our last-ditch effort to see if we could work as a family, and a massive failure. We could not. Because of that, I'd shunned the ocean - associating it with pain. What a stupid decision that was. The water was neutral. It was my ex who had caused the pain. To experience the massive waters again with a new love interest in the back of my mind was a completely different experience. I wondered what Caleb was doing. Thoughts of him coursed through me non-stop. *Was he thinking of me?* I wondered.

"Ouch!" I clenched my teeth against my mouthpiece in shock. Without warning, the waves had gotten rough again and knocked me into reef. It hurt like hell. *I need to get back to the boat.* I had been in my own world for too long and hadn't noticed that some others were already heading back. My arm stung as I swam back, and I noticed a thin trail of red in the water. Blood. Fuck! I panicked My skin had gotten scraped by the wallop of the sea and it set off alarm bells in my mind. *I need to get back to the boat!* I made my way back as fast as I could. I nearly fainted when I got there.

"Give me your hand!" Another passenger yelled before pulling me up.

Salt water whipped across my face while the undercurrent fought for my legs. *Shit!* I accidentally gave him the hurt hand and it throbbed with pain from his grip. I wanted to scream. God dammit, how did it go from glory to gruesome so fast? A trail of blood slid from the tip of my pinky to the base of my wrist.

"You alright?" The captain looked alarmed. He rushed over with a first aid kit.

"I'm okay," I assured. "I'm alright."

Meanwhile, several others were hurling vomit overboard. The excursion was rough, and we were all ready to go. That was enough adventure for me for one day. Even after I'd calmed down and we finally made our way back to shore, I couldn't shake the sight of my blood staining the water.

"You should get that looked at just in case," another passenger said. "Make sure it doesn't get infected," she added.

Oh, come on, I thought. I hadn't even considered that. "I will," I responded.

Hopefully she was wrong. It was just a scrape, well, maybe a gash. I didn't know how much of a difference it made that it was from underwater rocks with God knows what on them. It hurt though. Badly. And I just wanted to go back to my resort.

When we got back on land, I got help from my concierge finding a clinic, but they were closed for the day. I'd have to wait until the next morning, so I had to tend my own wound until then. I refused to go to the hospital as they suggested. That would have been overkill. Instead, I cleaned up, changed, took some aspirin, and took a nap. Saying I was exhausted was an understatement.

. . .

HOURS later I awaked to a video message from Caleb. It was a beautiful surprise to see his handsome face after the day I'd had. I'd planned on texting him that night anyway. I missed him.

Morgan, I wanted to drop you a quick message to let you know how much I've missed you while you've been away. The last two days have felt strangely empty without our lively conversations and your beautiful smile. I hope you're having fun in the Bahamas, but I can't deny that I'm looking forward to you coming back so I can see you again. Until then, take care and know that you've been on my mind. Catch you soon, gorgeous. Oh! Have a drink for me! He said with a smile and chuckle before ending his message.

I swooned! Caleb had a way of bringing out a teenage-like girl in me. He made my skin tingle and my heart race. I loved everything about his demeanor and easy-going, honest nature. Even his nerdy way of speaking. I called him back, but he didn't answer. Admittedly, I was disappointed. I wanted to talk to him live.

My hand hurt less, thank goodness, and at Caleb's request, I decided to go down to the bar and have a drink. It was only 8:00 pm., and I didn't have any other plans and didn't feel like leaving the property.

"Whiskey lemonade, please," I asked.

There were only a few other people there, mostly couples, one family with rambunctious kids and a solo female traveler with her head buried in her phone. The surrounding views were gorgeous. An infinity pool overlooking the Atlantic and a slowly descending sun drenching the sky in a rich mélange of gold and blue hues.

"Your drink, ma'am," the bartender reappeared with a glistening, gold-tooth accented smile. He was cute in a vagabond sort of way. A sharp jawline dotted by a scruffy beard. His hair was swept into a ponytail of locs while the sides were shaved down. "Thank you," I smiled.

He exuded an ease and fluidity with his movements. "My pleasure."

I sipped and people watched. The woman who just minutes before was glued to her phone screen was now scribbling in a journal while looking up every now and then to check out the ocean. She was interesting - feet crossed at the ankles below the table and fingers interlocked into a fist when not writing. *Why so closed?* I wondered. She was plump, wearing a tangerine swimsuit mostly covered by a blue and tan chiffon robe. She didn't look as happy as her color choices suggested.

"Another one," I downed my first drink faster than I thought I would. The slow burn of the alcohol coursing its way through my body was a balm to the tension I'd had. "Do you have any peach flavor you could add to it this time?" I flashed the young bartender a flirtatious smile.

He reciprocated. What the hell was I doing? I quickly stopped the urge to bite my bottom lip and initiate a full-on flirting session. It would have been so effortless. *Why not?* My inner voice egged me on. I didn't have a valid reason not to. Something felt different in me. Freer. Besides, it wasn't like I was in a relationship. Heck, Caleb himself said he didn't want to head in that direction so...*why not!?* Flirting was fun!

"Here you go," Nolan came back with my drink. I'd noticed his name tag this time. "What happened there?"

"Snorkeling accident."

"Sorry to hear that," he said. "Hope it doesn't hurt too badly."

"I'm fine, thank you." I sipped my new drink. "This is good!"

"I'm glad you enjoy it," Nolan's accent was a subtle melody. "That's not the only good thing around here." He winked. "If you need any recommendations for a good time, just let me know, you know, okay? I am happy to help!" He charmed.

Before I could answer, my phone lit up with a notification from my daughter.

It's so beautiful here! Her message came through with photos from her trip to Costa Rica. *Just checking in to let you know I'm okay. Don't move too fast with that new guy!*

I almost cackled out loud! The parent-child tables had definitely

turned! I'd mentioned to Simone a few weeks ago that I'd met someone. Well, it's more like she detected a change in my tone and
guessed it.

I'm glad you're enjoying yourself! Also, mind your business, I
responded. I was grateful for her message though. It prompted me to
close out my tab so I could go to my room and call Caleb. I
missed him.

I thanked Nolan for his offer to give me tips and finished my
drink. "I'll take the check now," I said. Nolan's hands grazed mine
when he took my debit card. Between his touch and the alcohol, I felt
my hormones building up in desire.

He looked directly into my eyes. "Anytime, beautiful. Have a good
evening."

It was time to go!

CHAPTER 8

I shed my clothes for a hot shower when I reached my room. My hand had started aching again, so I took a few aspirin hoping the pain would subside. As the water washed over my skin, I thought of Caleb. I wished he were in the shower with me. Immediately after that desire became known, I realized I was curious about how he looked without clothes. He'd said that he'd transitioned more than two decades before and still took testosterone to maintain. I guessed that meant he looked every bit as biologically male as possible. And, I imagined, I would find out soon because I wanted him.

The more I lathered my skin with soap and water, the more thoughts of being with him aroused me. I got wet. There was a clear distinction between the water from the shower head and me. I got hot. Beyond the steam, my temperature rose, and I exhaled slowly— almost panting as I felt a new throb build between my legs. It had been so long since I'd felt this because of someone else. I washed myself quickly, wanting to get out to call him.

After my shower, I dried off, settled in the bed in my hotel room, and dialed Caleb's number, eager to connect with him.

"Morgan! Look at you gracing me with a phone call. I was starting to think my video might have been too much...or that you were so captivated by my charm that you'd become speechless." He jumped right into a conversation.

"Don't flatter yourself. Your message was the highlight of my day, though. You always know how to leave an impression."

"My message was the highlight? Really? How's your vacation going?"

"It could be better. The water was choppy today. We shouldn't have gone out, but we did, and I hurt my hand. I'm gonna get it looked at tomorrow."

"Ouch. That bad?"

"I don't think so. I hope not. I'm just being cautious to ensure I don't get an infection or anything."

"Damn. I'm sorry to hear that. Really, I am."

"Thank you."

"It sounds like you should come home; I mean...I make a pretty good house call nurse."

"Is that right?"

"I have no idea," he laughed, "but I'd like to apply for the job if you need one. I miss you."

He took my breath away. "I miss you too." Talking to him always felt so effortless. No guessing at his thoughts. No frustration from him not speaking in complete sentences like most men I'd dated. Caleb was expressive, and I was enthralled by him.

"So, what are you doing now?"

"Laying here. Naked. Putting on lotion as I talk to you, actually. I just got out of the shower."

"Oh..."

"I um...I kept thinking of you as the water poured over me."

"So, I'm not the only one having those thoughts?"

"Absolutely not. I wondered how it would be if you were in there with me." I confessed as I finished moisturizing my legs. I lay on my back in the bed to get more comfortable.

"It would be ecstatic. And a relief."

"Relief?"

"Yes," he admitted. "I've been fantasizing about you since our first kiss."

I squirmed at the thought of him desiring me for so long. "Tell me more."

"Well, your lips were just so soft. So perfect. I knew you were eager and nervous at the same time, but when we connected at that moment, I could feel your anxiety melting away. It was clear that our chemistry wasn't purely intellectual. It was physical, and I felt you soften into the moment. I noticed your breathing go from fast and shallow to measured and deep."

"You noticed all of that?" I was genuinely surprised, especially about my breath.

"I did. I paid attention to every signal your body gave so I could know how to better touch you if you gave me more chances. Since then, I've been thinking about how I would explore the geography of your body, exploring every inch to discover the spots and sensations that make you come alive through pleasure."

"I would love that. Honestly, it's been too long since I've lost myself in passion with someone else." My cheeks flushed as I spoke.

Caleb's voice lowered, filled with a mixture of longing and intimacy. "Morgan, there's so much about you that captivates me. Your courage, your honesty, your vulnerability, your adventurous spirit, and the way you've embraced going on a journey to find what makes you happy at this point in your life versus settling for a picture of success. I really want to explore every facet of who you are, both in and out of the bedroom. And I want to create unforgettable memories together, ones that will keep us craving each other even in the quietest moments—whether we're in the same room or not."

"Caleb..."

"If I were in that bed with you right now, I'd dedicate at least twenty minutes to intentionally exploring your body with my lips, tongue and fingertips."

"I wish you were here. My body is craving your touch. Your energy. It's like my skin is already responding to just your words. I feel connected to you. I want you."

"Connection is everything. It's where the deepest sexual fulfillment is. That's why I want to take my time with you. To get to know your body. Where to touch you. How much pressure to use. When to go deeper. When to back off. I want to dance with you in the most intimate and intense way, Morgan."

"You're starting to right now." I felt wetness building up between my legs.

Every word Caleb spoke made my body pulse with new energy. I wanted to push forward and talk dirty to him, but I had no idea what to say because he was the first trans person I'd dated. I didn't want to overthink it, but I couldn't help but be nervous about sounding like a fool. He looked, walked and talked like any other man, but I didn't know what was under his hood. Well, no. . . he didn't speak like *any* other man I'd met. Caleb was in a league of his own, and I loved it. But what should I say? How far should I go? It didn't help that I always felt silly doing phone sex. But this time was different. I wanted to.

"How does your body feel?" he asked, as if he knew I needed help.

"Intense. Wanting. . . warm, wet and throbbing," I tried. "Yours?"

"Relaxed but also wanting. Wanting to feel the heat of yours pressed against mine. Wanting to feel your breasts against my chest. Wanting to graze my thumbs over your nipples until they harden under my touch."

Harden. The word stuck out like a thorn in silk. There was an unexpected silence, a rarity in our usual fluid conversations.

"Is something wrong?" he asked.

"Not really. I just," I paused to gather my thoughts. I wanted to speak cautiously and not ignorantly. "Caleb, I am enjoying every second of every moment I spend with you..."

"But?"

"But I've never been with a trans guy before, and we haven't discussed that much physical stuff, and I don't know what to say because I don't want to say the wrong thing. I don't know what your body looks like," I rambled.

"Mm." Caleb took a beat, his voice steady and reassuring. "Fair enough. I understand."

I exhaled in relief. I needed guidance.

"I have all the parts you're used to. They work the same way," Caleb spoke confidently, putting me at ease. "I had bottom surgery years ago, and I can give you the deep, powerful thrusts to rival anyone you've been with before me because I'm a different kind of man."

Well damn! "Okay."

"Don't worry, Morgan. I know the intricacies of a woman's body in a way that a cis, hetero man can't. And I'm patient, willing and eager to understand your specific needs. Even though this is new for you, I'll do everything I can to avoid making it awkward."

"Thank you." Our conversation was spellbinding. "I love your energy."

"I want to embed myself in yours."

The intensity of his words brought a comforting warmth, like the smooth caress of whiskey against the lips. At that moment, I knew that our connection was something extraordinary that transcended physicality and ventured into the realm of a deep and passionate bond. I put him on speakerphone to free my hand and touch myself. I didn't speak. I only deepened my breaths. There was something about what followed that couldn't be captured in words. As I moved my hand over my stomach, over my breasts, and up to my neck, I heard him breathing harder.

"Open your legs," he whispered, and I did. "I want to kiss down your thighs to your calves to your feet. Slowly. Gently."

My body trembled. Slow gyrations built from my hips, and my fingertips found their way to my aching, dripping...center.

"Are you stroking?" I asked.

"Very much," he exhaled.

I teased my clit, thinking of him caressing his erection. "I can't wait to feel you inside me." My body softened, feeling more open and welcoming.

He moaned, sending me to another height of arousal. Caleb and I lingered in the space on the edge of bliss for as long as we could stand it.

The intensity of our connection seemed to keep deepening. As I touched myself in ways I hadn't done in months, I felt a sense of tenderness and limitless possibilities. If Caleb had me this open over the phone, I could only imagine the level of passion we'd exchange in person. We worked ourselves up to the point of thunderous releases and a quiet pillow talk until we struggled to stay awake.

"Get some rest," I told him. My eyelids were barely open.

"I will. I can't wait to see you."

"I'll be back soon."

"Good night." I could tell he was smiling.

"Good night, Caleb." I disconnected the call and slipped into a series of wet dreams.

THE NEXT TWO days felt like a dream. I ended up not going to the clinic for my hand because it felt much better. Instead, I enjoyed the sun-drenched Bahamian beaches and crystal-clear waters. I felt so carefree. So young. So rejuvenated. It was glorious. As my time in paradise drew to a close, I grew excited about finally seeing Caleb again. We texted a lot, stoking the remaining embers from our connection. Now, I sat on the plane bound for Atlanta, feeling as giddy as a school-aged girl with a crush.

CHAPTER 9

Because of scheduling conflicts, Caleb and I couldn't see each other right away. He lived outside the city, and I was slammed with back-to-back in-person and virtual meetings for several days. As much as I desired him, it had to wait until the weekend. Amidst my whirlwind schedule, an unexpected sighting breathed a wild pause in the chaos. I sat in my car, idling at a traffic light in bustling Buckhead, and a flicker of recognition broke my thoughts. My eyes were drawn to a figure across the street, and a glimmer of familiarity sparked within me. *Is that...No, it couldn't be him.* I shook my head negatively. *No way!*

I strained to get a clearer view. The light changed, and as I drove past him, our eyes locked in a moment of mutual astonishment. Mine felt like they would pop out of my head, unable to comprehend the sight before me. There he stood—Nolan, the charismatic bartender from the Bahamas, on the other side of the street. His brow furrowed as he caught a glimpse of me as if he were in just much shock to see me as I was him! What the hell was he doing in Atlanta? Where was he going? I had so many questions, but I couldn't turn around. Or could I?

Lately, I had been seizing life by the reins, embracing spontaneity and following my desires without hesitation. The pull of curiosity intensified, tempting me to make a daring decision. *What about Caleb?* I glanced in my rear-view mirror, stealing a glimpse of Nolan's silhouette fading into the distance. *Should I turn around and say hi or keep going?* Caleb was the one who made it clear he didn't want just one woman, so why shouldn't I go back and maybe flirt a little? The fleeting seconds ticked away, each one a battle between my curiosity and cautious voice of reason. Ultimately, my foot pressed the accelerator, and I chose to keep going. Not every question gets an answer, and whatever Nolan was doing in Atlanta had nothing to do with me.

WHEN THE WEEKEND ROLLED AROUND, I found myself on a road trip to Treutlen County, Georgia—about three hours east of Atlanta—to see Caleb at his farm. The drive unfolded in a symphony of emotions, the quiet hum of the road matching my steady heartbeat. Each passing mile brought me closer to a reunion tinged with anticipation and an undercurrent of anxiety. How does Caleb live? Will I be completely isolated? Will our connection strengthen, or will seeing him in his element be too much for me? As I continued my drive east, dozens of questions unfurled along with the open roads. I mean, this man said he had an adult playroom in his house. Was I ready for all of that? We'd soon find out.

I arrived at a dirt hill road flanked by trees and tranquil garden scapes. It was expansive, with a southern gothic-inspired farmhouse as the focal point at the end of the road. The whole scene reminded me of a Richard Misrach photo. A barn stood adjacent to the farmhouse, weathered by time and carrying the weight of stories untold. I hadn't visited a farm since I took my daughter apple-picking when she was a little girl. Stepping out of my car onto the dirt road felt strangely refreshing. I instinctively inhaled, closing my eyes and feeling a light breeze on my skin. The air carried the scent of earth and echoes of nature's chorus. Birds rustling in the bushes, the wind and windchimes; it was as if the surroundings themselves harmonized with whatever mysteries were inside Caleb's house.

"Hey there!" Caleb called from his porch. He made his way to me expeditiously. Jovially. "Morgan!" A grin spread across his face as I walked closer to him.

"Hey, Caleb!" It felt like months had passed, but it had only been two weeks. Looking into his eyes was hypnotizing.

Without wasting another moment, we stepped into a deep, lingering embrace. He kissed my neck, ending it with a gentle bite before whispering in my ear, "I couldn't wait to see you again."

His hunger for me made blood race through my veins. I felt light on my feet and woozy from his tongue and teeth touching my flesh. "I missed you too," I finally managed to say.

"Come on in. Let me show you around. Did you find the place okay?" He took my hand and led me forward.

"I did. It was an easy drive." I glanced around as we walked forward.

"This was my great, great grandparent's property. It was actually bigger, but my cousins sold their shares years ago."

"Wow! You're so lucky to inherit something like this."

"Thank you. I realize that. I almost sold my parcel too, but I came to my senses and realized how valuable it was."

"Why didn't you want it?"

"I didn't want to live all the way out here. I wanted to be closer to the city. In the middle of more action, but after experiencing that for a few years while this sat vacant, I realized I was better off out here, even if I was alone."

"Interesting."

We strolled and spoke. He showed me where he grew Vidalia onions, which apparently were in high demand in gourmet cooking circles. Caleb also grew spinach, kale and lettuce. I'd arrived late afternoon on a Saturday, so none of his workers were there.

"The greens get planted in late spring, right after we harvest the onions," he explained. "I keep a steady rotation to maximize the land. I've grown everything from carrots and beets to radishes, tomatoes and peppers. Once I figured out what sold the most, I focused on those and kept small plants for my personal use."

"Do you sell most of it locally?"

"I do. I feed most of this town," he chuckled. "And I have deals with some of the private clubs in Atlanta. Over here," he pointed, "are my herbs," Caleb's voice filled with pride. "I've got basil, rosemary, thyme, and mint."

"Well, you've already proved you know your way around a kitchen."

"I just love creating beautiful experiences, and food hits the same pleasure zone as sex, so it's natural that I'd want to master the kitchen as much as I wanted to dominate the bedroom."

Dominate?

"Wrong word," he looked embarrassed when he saw my facial response. "I mean, I can dominate in the bedroom but not all the time, and that was very inappropriate for me to say. Fuck! I'm sorry." For the first time, Caleb seemed nervous and uncomfortable.

"It's okay." I know how it feels to have a *why the hell did I say that* moment. It happens.

"Uh...want to see inside now?" He tried to smile, but it was brief and tight.

"Sure."

"Okay, great!"

We entered through a backdoor that led directly to his kitchen and open living space. *Oh my!* I thought when we stepped inside. It was huge, inviting and more contemporary than I'd imagined. His kitchen was the focal point, and I could see his YouTube studio setup. Lights, a laptop, tripod, and microphone. Caleb's living room had a comforting touch of masculinity—oversized leather sofas, a wooden table adorned with big photography books and small metal sculpture accents. I looked closer and realized they were statues of male and female physiques. Soft ambient lighting illuminated specific locations in his living room, while other areas seemed to have strategic, gentle shadows.

"Did you design this place yourself?"

"I wish! I'm afraid my talents don't extend to interior decorating," he laughed. "I hired someone."

"Got it. It's beautiful. I love your fireplace." It had gray bricks above it, contrasting the butter-soft leather couches.

Caleb had a mix of books, bottles and baubles on the shelves. From yin and yang symbols to a lotus flower and intertwined figures —Caleb even had a tiny telescope next to a few vintage books. It was a beautiful blend of modernity and antiquity.

"You have an amazing home. It's so multifaceted and engaging... enchanting, actually. Just like you." I stepped closer to him. I wanted to be in his energy field and feel the heat from his skin.

He slipped his arm around me. "Let me show you the bar. Do you want something to drink, by the way?"

"Yes, I would. Thank you. Surprise me!"

He bit his bottom lip. "Hmm. Okay." Caleb had relaxed from his earlier faux pas, and it showed. "How about a Sensual Elixer? It's an Old-Fashioned spin-off, and I think you'll like it since we both love whiskey."

"I'm open."

"Perfect. Now. . . I am not a bartender, but I'll do my best!" Caleb was sure to temper my expectations.

His drink area was sleek, with an impressive whiskey and crystal glassware collection. I watched as he muddled a sugar cube and orange bitters in a mixing glass until the sweetener dissolved. He tossed soft ice in the glass and poured the whiskey before stirring it until it was chilled and properly diluted.

"Wait until you see this!" he said excitedly, pulling an ice tray from a mini freezer."What?" I didn't understand what could be so thrilling about ice.

But it wasn't regular ice. They were perfect molds of diamonds instead of regular cubes. He dropped a large one in a crystal glass and poured the strained cocktail over it. His attention to detail was impeccable. Caleb added a few more drops of orange bitters to the drink before twisting an orange zest and dropping it in the glass. "I hope you like oranges," he laughed.

"I love them!" At this point, I didn't want the drink, I wanted him. But I took a sip. "Whew! This is strong, but I like it."

Caleb beamed. "Bring it with you. I want to show you the front of the house and my room."

I did as he asked and watched Caleb pour the remainder of the drink into a flask. "Why are you drinking out of that?" I giggled.

"I have no idea. It just sits here, so I figured I'd use it. Does it give me character?"

"You don't need any help with that!" I slapped him playfully and took another tiny sip of my drink.

CALEB PATIENTLY SHOWED me the rest of his home, pointing out art he'd picked up from galleries and flea markets. He had a framed poster of "The Pale Blue Dot," a famous speech by Carl Sagan in his library, and an endless string of surprise elements. As we made our way to his bedroom, my anticipation built up. The door swung open, revealing a sanctuary of comfort and allure. Tapestries with rich earthy tones decorated the walls – it was almost bohemian – an unexpected departure from the rest of his house.

The room's centerpiece was a luxurious, king-sized bed dressed in crisp, white linens. The bed was elegantly minimalistic, with just a few carefully arranged pillows in neutral tones. Its simplicity spoke of Caleb's refined taste and a desire for uncomplicated elegance. On one side of the room, a vintage wooden vanity stood elegantly. Above it was a giant mirror that captured the room's essence.

"Is your bed firm or soft?" The words tumbled out of my mouth before I could stifle them.

"Firm," he smiled. "I sit in my reading nook if I want something soft under my butt," he joked and gestured to another corner.

I couldn't help myself. I grabbed his ass and squeezed.

He took a swig from his flask and looked me directly in my eyes. I took a bigger sip from my drink, then visibly let my tongue roll over the diamond ice. Caleb took the drink from me and put it down—

along with his—on a side table. "Come here," he said, and picked me up with both arms, so my legs were wrapped around his waist.

Caleb carried me to the chair in his reading nook. He placed me down gently and sat at my feet, taking one foot in his hand and running his fingertips up my calves. Once there, he pressed decisively, releasing tension. My body gradually fell limp as he did the same to my other leg. Eventually, Caleb made his way back to my feet and rubbed them. He leaned in and planted a slow kiss on top of each. My head fell back in relaxation. Between the drink and his touch, I sank into a space of *being*—a space of unobstructed *experiencing* and awareness of every single touch and breath. In that moment, sinking to a realm of attentiveness I'd never faced, I felt a surge of connection building between us. It was electric.

Caleb controlled the evening's pace like an orchestra conductor. He heightened the tension and then brought it down repeatedly—so much so that we eventually ended up back in his living room half-dressed and fully intoxicated. He brought out trays of light foods—passionfruit, black grapes, cherries, chocolate-dipped strawberries, cucumber slices—and we took turns serving each other until he pulled me to the floor, where we kissed, talked and rolled around to experience the feathery texture on our bare skin.

"I can't take it anymore," I finally confessed. "I want to go back upstairs. To your bedroom."

His gaze bore into me, connecting with the needs of my soul. "Come," he beckoned, and I obeyed.

My heart quickened, climbing to a rapid tempo under Caleb's lead. We ventured back to his bedroom and quickly tore off the rest of our clothes. My eyes were drawn to the contours of his chest, noticing scars, somewhat thin but present enough to be faded whispers etched across his skin. They told a quiet story of courage and transformation. They reminded me of personal challenges he'd face, battles he'd fought and triumphs he'd achieved in pursuit of living true to his soul. I found them strangely beautiful because of what they meant.

"May I?" I wanted to trace the delicate ridges with my fingertips.

"Yeah," it's okay. "There are no parts of my body that you can't explore. You?"

"I...I don't know. I haven't thought about it in a while."

"Well, just let me know if I touch somewhere you don't like, okay?"

"Of course." I noticed a giant scar on his leg and asked him about it.

"Well, that. That's um...the donor site of the skin used to complete my bottom surgery."

It took several moments for me to process what he'd said. I didn't get it at first, but soon, I realized he meant a skin graft. I didn't want to press and ruin the moment, so I let his simple answer be enough.

He pulled me onto the bed, on top of him, as he lay on his back. Caleb's hands palmed my ass, squeezing, gripping and pulling it apart as he thrust upward. I tossed my head to one side to get my locs out of the way and pressed my body into his, rotating my hips, enjoying the impact of his light smacks on my skin. The bulge in his pants was consistent. It felt good, yet I wondered how it would grow. I was so clueless but tried not to overthink.

Caleb soon unfastened my bra and rolled us over, so he was on top. He kissed both sides of my neck, across my collarbones, my shoulders and down to my breasts. As he explored my body, I sensed him playing with his own. He breathed heavier as he sucked and bit my sides, licked my stomach and tugged at my panties with his teeth. The room was almost quiet except for our groans, sighs and faint music. Caleb sat upright to fully undress me, and that's when I noticed his full erection through his boxers. Whatever he'd done to get up was so swift and discreet that it felt completely natural. I immediately sat up to pull his sex out so I could suck it. I was hungry for it.

His wood popped out easily, and I took in my mouth with ease. Caleb's leg shook at my sudden aggression. I surprised myself, but I shouldn't have. Everything about this man had me intrigued from the day we'd met. And now, I caressed his slight scatter of pubic hair while tracing the tip of his dick with my tongue in between sucking and stroking him. My body leaked with the sticky wetness of arousal. Our passion was intense, rising and falling like waves in an endless ocean. Caleb thrust in my mouth, continuing to build before gently pulling back and out. He lay me back down and placed his warm hand over my vulva, eventually lifting all but his thumb and middle fingers, which he used to caress my lips. Caleb rubbed and squeezed with a feather soft-touch. He used his thumb to tease me with a circular motion.

"Is that pressure good?" He asked.

"Yes..." I breathed.

"Can I press harder? Or do you want me to keep it right there?"

I didn't know. "Uh...yeah, press harder..."

He gazed at me compassionately while upping the power of his touch. He surprised me by slowing down with intensity rather than speeding up, and before I knew it, he was teasing the entrance to my sex with another finger while still rubbing my clit. I gushed, both audibly and physically. I could feel my wetness sliding to the sheets beneath me.

"I love how you smell," he said before kissing my inner thighs. Caleb slid his finger in me a few times before pulling out deliberately and slowly. He used the same hand coated with my essence to massage my legs down to my feet.

My body rocked. Our lust seemed to create a unique rhythm and flow that was both thoughtful and spontaneous at the same time. I wanted Caleb to go down on me so badly, but he licked everywhere but there. He kissed me a few times but moved his attention back to my lips, thighs and stomach. He flipped me over and dragged his nails down the center of my back. I felt his hard dick pressing against my ass, telling me to thrust backward and encourage him to rub against me more. I arched my back and lifted my body to give him greater access, and without missing a hint, he grabbed me by the hips and let his shaft rub against my wet pussy from the back. I wanted it inside.

"Caleb, please...fuck me," I begged. My body burned with desire.

He pressed me back flat on the bed and lay on me at length, his rod nearly sandwiched between my cheeks, and whispered in my ear. "Soon. I waited too long for this. I want it to last."

I protested inwardly, even though I felt amazing and alive. Our bodies danced and entangled in the sheets. Finally, he pulled me onto his face and unleashed the power of his tongue on my hungry wet flesh.

"Oh my god..." I sang, while grinding, riding and feeding him. It felt so good that I lost myself in a moment of complete abandon.

Caleb hummed while he ate, creating a vibrating sensation that sent my body into a tailspin. I nearly collapsed from pleasure. He paused to turn me around so I could ride his face while he played with himself. I eventually laid down on his chest, close enough to take him in my mouth again. I felt him relax beneath me, enjoying the warmth my enveloping tongue provided him. Eventually, I repositioned myself to face him again.

He moved me to the front of a spooning position and reached over me for something in his nightstand. Lube. "We don't need it now because you're wet enough, but I like to have it right there just in case," he said, and pulled out one more thing. A condom. He tore off the package and slipped it on before instantaneously pushing inside me from the back.

"Whew, yes!" My body shuddered with gratitude and hedonistic euphoria.

Caleb pumped me at a moderate pace, cupping his arm underneath mine to help him better cling to me from the back.

"Harder," I whispered.

"Yeah," he ramped up. "You want it harder? Tell me again."

"Harder!" I cried.

He plunged with more force, soon putting me on my stomach again to give it to me doggy style. He grabbed my hair as he stroked me intensely. So much so that his dick sometimes popped out and bounced against my ass before he stuck it back in. After a while, it was too much, and I needed a break. "Okay, okay," I said breathlessly, "slow down, please..."

He exhaled loudly. Tired, but still attentive. Gradually, he slowed down and pulled out—rubbing the head of his dick against my clit. I reached down to help him, sometimes slipping him back inside before pulling him out to rub up and down again. I did this over and over until I reached an irrepressible peak and let out an orgasmic scream. Bliss rippled over me like a warm cascade.

Caleb started moving again. "I just need a minute or two," he said, sliding back inside me.

I was throbbing and ready to roll over, but I knew I needed to give him time to climax. He slid in and out easily for a few strokes before asking, "Do you mind if I use something extra? Nothing out there," he comforted.

"Go for it."

He grinned and got up to retrieve two small, leather floggers. "Have you experienced these?"

"No, do they hurt?"

"Not at all—unless you want them to. But I don't want to hurt you."

"Okay. What do you want me to do?"

"Just lay there for now." He held one in each and hand, and traced the contours of my skin with the leather tassels. It felt amazing and revitalized me faster than I thought I could be. "I'm going to whip your skin just a little bit, is that okay?"

"Yes." I trusted him.

"Alright..." he said while slowly moving each hand in a circular – wax on, wax off moment. "Just say 'stop,' if you want me to," Caleb added before using each flogger in a fluid, coordinated motion that impacted my breasts and stomach. It looked like art and felt like heaven.

The sting of the contact hurt in a good way and brought a new flow to our intimate dance. "Can I try it on you?" I was curious. "I have no idea what I'm doing, but it looks fun," I confessed.

Our exchange suddenly became more playful, even with laughs at my expense and sexual naivete. I loved how we effortlessly kept our passion going by nurturing and nourishing it without fear of embarrassment. Right then, I made a mental note of feeling proud of myself. Caleb brought out a whole new me, and I didn't run from her. It felt like our possibilities might be endless. We soon took a break to refuel on light bites and drinks—talking and getting to know each other even more between our sessions. Time seemed to stand still, and the outside world melted away. We even dozed off at some point. Caleb gently woke me back up by rubbing his dick against my lips. I was taken aback but indulged. I sucked it while waking up, which seemed to send him over the edge. His eyes rolled back, and his body tensed as he released a thunderous, pent-up orgasm.

"There you are," I smiled as he pulled back, his body still shaking. "I hope that was as good as it sounded."

"It was better!" He fell backward on the bed and motioned for me to lay in his arms. As I did, he reached down to—I assume—do whatever he did earlier but to deflate his erection.

That was the first time in a long time I'd had sex with the lights on. I think it was the only time I'd been with someone and felt so safe, curious and liberated. Caleb was a taste of nirvana, and I wanted seconds.

CHAPTER 10

"Where did you get this shirt?" I cackled in amusement. "I don't know. Some street festival," he giggled. "It looks good on you!"

The shirt read, *you can't be boring and bad in bed, pick a struggle!* "It's perfect for you though. You are the most intellectually *and* physically stimulating person I've ever been with in my life. And to think of how much I judged and side-eyed you for wearing yellow Crocs the day we met!"

"Appearances can be misleading, baby girl. I bet you learned your lesson now!"

"Oh hush. You were also wearing hoochie daddy shorts," I pushed him playfully.

"Made you look though!"

Caleb and I had whirled in the throes of passion for hours the night before and woke up just after 10:00. He'd lent me one of his t-shirts and sweatpants to wear around the house because somehow, I didn't think to pack an overnight back even though I knew he lived almost three hours away. Of course, it would be too late, and I'd be too tired to drive back home the same night.

"Life's mostly a game to me," Caleb said. "I do what I want, wear what I want, and act how I want most of the time."

"That sounds so free!"

"It is! Don't you think that's how life is supposed to be?"

"Yeah, but it's never been so simple for me."

"Well, in my mind, as long as I'm not hurting other people, there's no reason for me to conform to what everyone else thinks is right or normal." He gestured for me to have a seat at the kitchen island and pulled out a few glasses.

"How did you get to this point? I mean, between parents, social expectations, and cultural pressures, it's not easy...especially with you being trans, right?"

"It was hard at first, but being trans basically gave me two choices: conform and be miserable, or rebel and take whatever good and bad came with living life on my terms."

"Hm." I drank in his words.

A silence hung over us as he busied himself to prepare a simple breakfast. I watched as he buzzed about the kitchen, taking a moment to turn music on using his phone as a remote control.

"What song is this?" My ears perked up at the gentle piano melodies and subtle acoustic textures.

"Kevin Garrett, 'In Case I Don't Feel,'" Caleb answered.

"Never heard of him, but I like it."

"It's a little melancholy, but I still like the vibe and instrumentation." Caleb placed a plate of avocado toast topped with a fried egg and cherry tomatoes before me. "Bon appétit!"

"Thank you." I was starving!

"You're welcome," he offered as he fixed a plate of his own and sat in front of me. "Anyway, back to what we were talking about earlier; I don't take myself or other people too seriously."

"I'm getting there. I used to take everything too seriously. I thought if I controlled people's perception of me, I'd have greater control of my life."

"And what did that get you?"

"Money. Power. Respect..."

"And?"

"Loneliness. Confusion about who I am and what I want. I worked so hard to be perfect that I didn't know what authentic looked or felt like. Except for my hair," I laughed. "That's probably the only rebellious thing up until recently."

"I love your hair. The way some of your locs fell from your pony-tail and dangled over me while you rode me last night was beautiful. Your body is gorgeous. I don't think I told you that."

"Thank you." I finished my toast. "So…"

"So?"

"There's an elephant in this room, Caleb."

He chortled. "What is that?!"

"I don't think I got the full house tour yesterday," I said.

"Ohhhh," he leaned back with flushed cheeks. Caleb suppressed a smile and almost looked like a meme. "Aha."

"Your…playroom?"

"You're right. I didn't want to spring too much on you too soon," he laughed. "Are you sure you want to see it?"

"Yes! You can't tell someone you have an adult rumpus room and *not* show it to them. The hell is wrong with you?"

"Okay, then, damn! I was taking it easy on you! Come on." He got up and gestured for me to follow him. "It's right here," he smiled devilishly pulling a book on his bookshelf forward to reveal a secret room.

What the fuck?

"If I'd put it in the basement, it would have come off as creepy. I didn't want to do that," Caleb explained, reading my mind.

"Fair enough."

Caleb left the door open behind us and flicked a switch that turned on red LED lights. "Hold on," he said, and pressed the control pad a few times until it turned to regular white lights. When he first told me he had an adult playroom, my mind somersaulted to red alert, and there I was about to walk right into it. A sign reading, "Welcome to the Dungeon" adorned one of the walls and my eyes nearly popped out of my head. I didn't realize I'd also mouthed the words out loud.

Caleb turned around with genuine concern. "Please don't be intimidated by that. I purposely didn't call it that because I didn't want to scare you. I didn't know how you'd respond. I promise it's not whatever you thought a sex dungeon might look like."

"Caleb, I swear to God, I have *never* wondered what a sex dungeon might look like!" I gulped and looked behind me. Okay, great. The bookcase door was still open in case I needed to make a beeline out. *Who the fuck has a sex dungeon in their home? Does he have a white van with no windows like my mother used to warn me about?* My mind tumbled into fearful and judgmental questions. *Calm down. Give it a chance.* I coerced myself to relax as we walked further in.

"I took the best ideas from luxury hotels, high-end bars and combined them with the dark beauty of dominance and submission play," Caleb explained as we walked into the main space.

The walls were black and accented with extravagant gold accents. He had crown molding, a striking, tufted black leather couch and ice cube shaped table. There were shelves with candles, framed erotic art and a few small bottles of whiskey. In one corner was a massage table that looked like it was in a shower.

"What is going on over there?" I pointed.

"That's for slippery and wet fun. I love giving different kinds of massages, but the oils can make a mess. I don't want it ruining the furniture, so that area is for any kind of messy play."

"Okay."

"This," he pointed to a giant X thing, "is called a St. Andrews cross. It's great for a whole-body sensory experience."

I listened quietly, taking it all in.

Caleb was excited. "These drawers are for toy storage. This is a spanking bench. I actually haven't played in here in a while, but when I do, I prefer to have the lights soft and warm. I call it a dungeon, but I don't want it to feel like a grimy one. Oh, and over here," he pointed to what looked like another bookshelf. "Is my Murphy bed."

I just looked at him. He pressed a button on the wall and slowly, a bed came down.

"I didn't want to use a ton of space for this, so I maximized what I could. And that," he pointed to a corner next to the leather couch, "is something I think you'll love!"

"Oh really?" His giddy tone snapped me out of my trance.

"Yes, really!"

"What is it?" I had no idea what I was looking at.

"It's called a queening chair."

"A what?"

"Do you remember how you rode my face last night?"

"Yes..."

"Well, when you're ready, you can just have a seat in that chair, and I'll slide in under you. Same premise, except you don't have to worry about balance or holding yourself up. Just sit—like a queen—and enjoy!"

"Oh, Caleb!" I felt embarrassed.

"Too much?" he asked jovially.

"I don't know!" I searched for words.

"Well, that's it, Morgan. I promise." He looked at me hopefully.

I just blinked.

"Tell me what you're thinking. It can be anything."

"I'm thinking how you could have all this right off your dining room and there not be a clue. I'm wondering what kind of toys are in those drawers. I'm questioning if I'm intrigued, appalled or both. I'm speculating on how dominant you really want to be and if I'm ready. A lot, Caleb, I thinking a lot!" I laughed nervously.

He pulled me into a nearby embroidered leather armchair and said, "One, I don't have many people over these days. It's like I built this playroom when I barely have friends to play with," he laughed. "Two, I have a variety of toys. Candles, wands, small things here and there. And three, I think you're intrigued and want to play with me."

"You're so sure of yourself, and me."

"I try," he grinned. "And to be honest with you, I'm a bit of a switch."

"I don't know what that means, Caleb."

He sighed. "Right. You're vanilla."

"Shut up!" I playfully slapped his head.

"I'm only teasing. Look at you hittin' me already! You might have an inclination for BDSM for sure!" He laughed. "This is abuse!"

"That's not funny, Caleb," I giggled anyway.

We leaned back in relaxed amusement—me on his lap.

"I don't always want to dominate my lover is what I meant by switch. I don't mind leading, but I also get an intense amount of pleasure from relinquishing all control and submitting. Being a man is exhausting. I'm not afraid to say that out loud. Letting go of control allows my mind and muscles to take a break from constantly working. It lets me get lost in being and sensing. In trusting someone else."

I rubbed his chest, giving myself time to absorb his words. Without provocation, my hands wondered down his stomach to his pants. Caleb cleared his throat and exhaled. He reached for his phone to play music from built in speakers. A mesmerizing, ethereal song poured a new layer of energy into the atmosphere.

"What is this? You have the best music."

"Thank you. It's called 'Dive' by RAAHiim."

"It's hauntingly beautiful."

"Sort of like you."

"More like you. You're both an open book and a mystery. You excite me and make me nervous. I want to open up completely, but I'm scared."

"Of what?"

"The unknown. Myself. This is all so much. So new. So different. I'm sitting in a fucking sex dungeon with a trans man I met at a dingy gas station in the middle of nowhere Georgia. What is going on in my life?"

"Well damn, girl! You don't have to say it like that!" He laughed.

"Wearing god-awful lemon-colored Crocs and dueling with me over the last bottle of water. I don't know if I should have listened to my therapist. This is what I get for chasing childhood dreams," I goaded. "Out there stargazing one night and the next thing I know I'm sitting on your lap."

"Loving every second of it, aren't you? Be honest." He kissed me before I could answer. Caleb pulled off my shirt and hungrily took my breasts into his mouth, gently grazing his teeth against my nipples.

I felt drunk, and yes, loving it. I straddled him to give him better access to my body, kissing his forehead and temples—whatever I could reach as he devoured me. Caleb picked me up again and brought me to the wet area—where the massage table and shower were. My body vibrated in eagerness. The moment he put me down, I pulled off the pants I'd been wearing. He patted the table, and I climbed on top. Caleb then stripped down naked and began to slowly massage me, first with his hands and then his entire body. He climbed on the table and glided against me. I didn't even see him get any oil, but at some point, he must have. We were completely body to body.

"Is the temperature in here okay?" he whispered. "I meant to ask."

"Yeah, it's perfect."

"Good," he ran his tongue around the edge of my ear. "I need you completely stress-free."

"Mmmm." I moaned. My body began moving in its own euphoric rhythm against his.

He brought me into deep levels of relaxation with his touch and words. Caleb explored me with such focus and intention it made me wonder if I'd ever truly been made love to in my life. After a while, he carefully helped me off the table and turned on the shower. He held me a few steps back from the cascade of water to keep me warm while the flow heated up. Then, he proceeded to bathe me, and me him. We intuitively washed each other under the stream of droplets. It was in this moment I learned how Caleb's wood worked. In a moment of vulnerability, he showed me how he pumped it up to a full-hard on—a process identical to what cis hetero men with erectile disfunction use.

"Thank you for sharing more of yourself with me," I told him. I could only imagine how explaining that to me and previous women must have felt to him.

"I feel safe with you," he confided. "Do you feel safe with me?"

"Very much." I watched soap suds roll down his arms and fall off his fingertips. Gently, I lowered myself to the soft floors of the shower to taste him once more.

Caleb groaned as pleasure energy filled the room. We took turns tending to each other until we ended up back in the main dungeon area. It was the first time I'd been with anyone who didn't seem goal oriented—who wasn't constantly pushing towards an orgasm. My experience with him was more about discovery, learning each other second by second, and minute by minute.

We played and we talked. We ate and we dance. We fucked and we slept. The entire day was romantic, emotional and intellectual. Imaginative too. I wasn't ready to play with any of his dungeon furniture or delve into role play, but I imagined how it might be. We touched on it through talk instead of rushing into doing it, and I was grateful for that. Just visualizing how it might feel be tied up on the cross or bent over on the bench sent me to the lap of God. We talked dirty. Filthy. In ways that older versions of me would have cringed, but it set my soul on fire now. It awakened parts of me that I were asleep for too long, and some parts that I didn't realize I'd had.

"I'd love to give you all the power next time," Caleb told me. "I want you to take control. I want to submit to you in every way you can conceive, Morgan. Do you think you can handle that?"

"I don't know, but I'm willing to try."

"Tell me what to do. Where to put my face, my hands, my tongue...blindfold me and surprise me. Surprise yourself. Just let go!"

"That does sound thrilling."

"I'll be in complete servitude," he smiled. "I could use that."

I kissed him, already knowing that I would push myself to go through with it next time. Pandora's box was open, and I liked what fell out. Later that afternoon, I begrudgingly made the long drive home.

"Call me once you get on the highway. I'll keep you company on the drive," Caleb said as he walked me to my car.

"I will," I said, and pulled him into a deep embrace. "I will."

CHAPTER 11

The next few days found me blissfully living in the hazy afterglow of my weekend with Caleb. Work didn't even annoy me. My mind and body were at ease for the first time in a long time. I felt light and energized, waking up without an alarm clock and easily writing in my journal. I loved the flow of entries from my beginning to now. Therapy does work! I couldn't wait to see Caleb again, but it would have to wait another week or two, as he had travel plans, and I needed a weekend to myself for beauty maintenance and pampering.

The days went by slower than usual, but I didn't mind. Caleb and I used video chat to keep our nights steamy. Little did I know that amid the serenity and anticipation, a storm was brewing in the depths of the unknown. It was a bright, sunny morning when the ringing of my phone sliced through the tranquility like a thunderclap through calm. After I picked up the call, the voice on the other end delivered words that shattered my universe.

"Hello?"

"Hello, is this Morgan Carter?" The voice on the other end sounded firm and authoritative, carrying a weight that instantly made my heart gallop to attention.

"May I ask who's calling?"

"Of course. My name is Benjamin Alvarez, the estate attorney handling your father's estate case."

"Wait. What?" I was confused. I hadn't heard from my dad in more than 15 years. I barely knew who he was.

"I'm calling with heavy news, I'm afraid."

My head was spinning. In seconds, I went from nirvana to nightmare.

"Your father, Maurice Carter, recently passed away," he continued. "I offer my condolences, and I understand this may come as a shock. I'm sorry to be the bearer of bad news. It took us a little while to find you."

"We're not umm . . . we weren't close."

"Well, his last will and testament include an inheritance for you."

My breath caught in my throat as the weight of those words settled upon me. Time froze. Shock and a multitude of unanswered questions stampeded within me. "I . . . I don't know what to say," I finally managed to utter, my voice laced with confusion.

"I think it's best if we arrange a meeting to discuss the details."

"When did he die? How? Was there a service? Where's his body?" Questions gushed from me like a broken fire hydrant, and a mixture of emotions washed over me.

I'd distanced myself from my father more than a decade before because his fixation on perfection and religious piousness became toxic. He was overly judgmental and hypocritical—the kind of annoying Christian who said one thing in public but acted the opposite in private—unlike my mother, who truly embodied the words of Christ and lived them daily. No matter our relationship before she passed, I would never not credit her for trying to be an exceptional human being who always helped others. My dad, on the other hand, repressed a lot, drank a lot, cussed a lot, and constantly overstepped boundaries. Nothing I ever did was good enough for him. I couldn't stand him after a while. Never did I expect him to leave me an inheritance. I was surprised he had anything to leave, considering the path of substance abuse I remembered him traveling down. My world blurred with the sudden news.

"I'd be happy to share as many answers with you as I can. Do you have time this week to come in for a meeting? It's my job to guide you through the legal process."

"Where's your office?"

"Augusta. And it looks like you're in . . . Atlanta. Is that still correct?"

"Yes, it is. I can make time to come in on Friday," I told him.

"That's great, thank you. I can e-mail or text you the location. Look, I know this is a lot, but if it's any solace, I can tell you that your father noted in his papers his desire that you'd know he cared deeply for you."

My body deflated. In just a few minutes, one phone call snatched me out of my newfound bliss and dropped me into the shadows of my past. "Thanks. What time on Friday?" I asked, but my real question was how I would untangle the threads of unresolved emotions coming from parts of me that I'd buried long ago.

Benjamin and I coordinated a time for me to meet him at his office to discuss the details. When we hung up, I found myself in a strange domain of emotion. No tears flowed. No grief emerged, but years of unspoken words and unresolved conflicts bubbled up in me like a hot spring. Not long after, I took a deep breath and picked up my phone, my fingers trembling slightly as I searched for Caleb's number in my contacts. After a few rings, his face appeared on the screen, his eyes filled with concern the moment he saw mine. "Morgan, what's wrong?" he asked.

"Do I look that bad?" I tried to make light of the moment.

"No, but . . . you don't look so good. What happened?"

I hesitated, trying to find the right words. "Caleb," I began, my voice quavering. "I just received a call from my father's estate attorney. My dad passed away."

Caleb's expression softened, and he leaned closer to the screen, as if trying to offer comfort through the digital connection. "Oh,

Morgan, I'm so sorry. Are you okay? You've never mentioned him. Were you close?"

Tears welled up in my eyes as I shook my head. There they were. My raw emotions finally showed up. "I . . . I don't know how to feel, Caleb. We weren't close, and I haven't spoken to him in years. But it's still . . . a shock."

Caleb responded empathetically, "I can't imagine what you're going through, but I want you to know that I'm here for you. Whatever you need, I'm just a call away."

I let out a shaky breath, feeling a sense of relief knowing I had Caleb with me. "Thank you. Your support means the world to me."

His eyes held a mix of determination and vulnerability. "I may not have all the answers, but I promise to be as supportive as I can."

We talked a bit longer, and I shared more about my past with my father—how I'd felt inferior around him despite my success, and how the last time I saw him he was becoming an alcoholic who spent half his time in Medellín, Colombia, and the rest in Augusta, Georgia, where I grew up—partially—I'd also spent some years in Philly. I didn't tell Caleb about my inheritance. Heck, I didn't even know what it was. I figured I'd cross that bridge after I knew more. As we ended the call, I felt a renewed sense of comfort and strength.

Over the next few days, I found myself navigating the turbulent waters of grief and the complexities of my dad's death. Caleb remained a constant presence, offering words of encouragement and an ear whenever I needed to vent my emotions. Somehow, he understood the delicate balance between giving me space to process and being there for me when I needed his comforting presence. I appreciated his sensitivity and the way he held space for my pain without trying to fix it.

But as the days turned into weeks, I noticed a subtle shift in Caleb's demeanor. His messages became less frequent, and his responses seemed distant. I couldn't help but wonder if what I was going through triggered something within him, stirring up his own fears and insecurities. Our conversations that were once filled with passion and lighthearted banter now carried an underlying tension. I hadn't even seen him in person again because he'd gotten "busy."

One evening, as I mustered the courage to broach the topic, Caleb's voice sounded distant and detached. "Morgan, I've been doing some thinking," he began hesitantly. "I care about you deeply, but I need to be honest with you. I've always been someone who avoids commitment, and recent events have made me realize that I'm not sure if I'm ready for the kind of emotional investment you deserve."

You've got to be kidding me! "Are you breaking up with me? Right now?" My heart sank as his words hung in the air, a frigid breeze seeping into the warmth that had once enveloped us. I struggled to find my voice, my emotions a jumbled mess.

He interrupted gently, his voice tinged with regret. "I know how this might come off, Morgan. And I'm sorry. It's not a reflection of you or what we shared. It's about me and my own limitations. I thought you always wanted me to be honest with you."

He might as well have uppercut me. I did *not* see this coming! "Yeah, well, I appreciate your honesty, but it doesn't make it any easier. I thought we had something special."

Caleb was silent. There was a long pause before he spoke again. "I apologize. I know my timing is shitty. I know it hurts. And I know you expected more from me. And as much as it pains me to say this, I think it's what's best for you. For us."

"What's best for me?" Now I was pissed! "How the fuck are you going to break up with me after my father dies and say it's what's best for me?"

"You deserve better than me," is all he said, with heavy resignation in his voice.

This hurt more than anything. Why did he have to do this? Silence settled between us, a quiet acknowledgement of the disappointment that hung in the air.

"Bye, Morgan." He disconnected our call.

What the entire fuck?

CHAPTER 12

I couldn't make sense of the days that followed. The sudden news of my father's passing, coupled with Caleb's unexpected withdrawal, had left me feeling disoriented and bitter. It was as if the ground beneath me had given way, and I'd begun falling from light into a pit of hell. My heart was broken. My emotions were complex. I felt guilty about withdrawing from my father instead of being the bigger person and fighting harder to repair our relationship. I felt lost knowing that both my parents died young. I felt afraid that I might suffer the same fate. And I felt enraged that Caleb left me the way he did, even though I knew it was in character for him to be honest about his feelings. I just didn't think I'd be a victim to them, especially not like this. It hurt like hell.

My meeting with Benjamin Alvarez, my father's attorney, had shed light on my inheritance. It turns out that my Dad left me land, and shares of stock worth $160,000. All of a sudden, I owned 12 acres of property and had a mini financial windfall. It was a tangible reminder of our complicated relationship. I didn't think he liked me, but apparently, he still loved me to the end.

Then there was Caleb. My heart writhed in pain at the thought of him. Why did God even bring him into my life just to have him run away like that? What was the point? What was the purpose? That's why I had a hard time believing in God anyway.

I felt lost. Again. And as I walked the grounds of my inherited land, a mix of sadness and curiosity enveloped me. Twelve acres was a lot to me, a city girl who, besides stargazing at Deerlick and snorkeling on vacation, had rarely spent time in the vast expanse of nature. Why did my father even own this land? He was a philosopher and college professor—in what part of his life did he start buying random plots of land? What was I going to do with it? Lost in my thoughts, tears streamed down my cheeks as I sank to the ground. Everything hurt. My personal life felt like chaos, and I struggled to find meaning in any of it. The money was nothing to me.

The days blurred together with me grappling with regret, heartbreak, and heavy responsibility. I felt so alone and buried myself back into work—the one thing I'd felt so proud to escape perversely became my safe space. I could busy myself with meaningless meetings, tasks, and goals. I could temporarily hide from my turmoil in the aspirations of others. I could get lost in business travel and seeing new cities again, and I did. New York City. Memphis. Seattle. Sioux Falls. I traveled a lot, trying to escape all my feelings. But hiding from my pain was unsustainable.

On a mundane business trip, an unexpected realization hit me like a seismic wave of revelation. *Keep fighting.* I couldn't give up. I had to submit to reality while finding a way to flow with it versus getting knocked over by it—a glimmer of strength sparked within me. *Fuck Caleb!*

I had to forge my own path, find my own way forward. Even though it felt like someone put me in the spin cycle of a washing machine, I recommitted to finding happiness. I even reasoned that Caleb's tornado through my life might have been to teach me about honesty and enjoying moments and seasons with people. He never told me he wanted anything long-term. I assumed that. He never said he wanted anything deep and committed. I projected that. And to be honest, he never spoke deeply about his past or history—it was always just a good time. I saw more than there was because we were having fun. As I analyzed everything between us, a newfound resilience began blossoming in me. It still hurt, and I was still angry, but I acknowledged reality and tried to figure out what I'd do next.

Weeks into my struggle to find meaning and move forward, a courier package arrived at my building. "This is for you!" Tanya, my building's receptionist, smiled when she handed me a manila padded envelope over the counter.

"Thank you, Tanya." I smiled back, a much better human being to her than I used to be. No longer petty. No longer shallow. I'd been humbled by life in ways I'd never imagined.

"You are welcome. Have a blessed day." She nodded affirmatively and went back to typing on her phone.

The package felt flimsy, almost as if nothing were in it. I hesitated, unsure whether to open it or not because I didn't want any more negative surprises. The last thing I wanted was another blow to my already-fragile state of mind. Part of me wanted to toss it aside, to shield myself from any further pain, but curiosity got the better of me, as I couldn't read the packing slip. Once in my condo, I carefully tore open the package, revealing a small USB stick nestled inside with a note on brown stationery.

It was from Caleb.

My body collapsed. Anger welled in me again. But so did nosiness. A part of me wanted to throw it in the trash, while the other yearned to know what was on it. I sat there for several moments, my right leg and hand shaking. I wished he didn't have that effect on me. I wanted to hate him regardless of his technically not doing anything wrong. I wanted to jab my fists into his chest. I wanted to treat him like the punching bag he made me feel like when he broke up with me. But I also wanted to smell his cologne one more time. I wanted to share another deep conversation with him. *Fuck it*, I thought, and grabbed my laptop to insert the USB. There was only one file on it, and it was a video message.

Seeing his face again hastened my breath. His eyes reflected a vulnerability I had never seen before.

"I apologize, Morgan, for showing up like this, but I didn't have the heart to call you real-time. But if you would please, please, just watch this for the next few minutes, it would mean the world to me. I know I hurt you, and you don't owe me anything, but if there's even the smallest bit of connection to me left in you, I ask that you please . . . hear me out," he began. Caleb looked down, unable to hold eye contact with the camera. He looked nervous and helpless.

"I ran away because I was scared," he continued, his voice filled with emotion. "Scared of the depth of my feelings. Scared of what you triggered in me. And scared of commitment. The truth is, Morgan, I pretend that I don't want a committed relationship, but I really do," he confessed. "I act like I'm incapable of being with one person, but I really can—as long as clear communication is there, and that person is willing to explore life with me and not make me feel weird. Since we've been apart, I've realized I was only fooling myself by thinking what I did was the right thing to do. It wasn't. It was a dick move, and I can't say I'm sorry enough. I never meant to hurt you. I never meant to leave you when you needed me the most, and I never meant to be the kind of man who would pretend to be something he's not just because he's too afraid to look inside and get to the root of his feelings."

I'd never seen or heard such a raw display of emotion. Caleb's eyes now filled with tears as he continued speaking.

"I'm so sorry! I regret my actions, and I've felt tortured every day we haven't spoken." He took a beat. "I've missed you like I've never missed anyone. That's why I'm sending this. I wish I had the courage to do it in person, but I feel so guilty for how I handled things, so I thought this was the best way to get through it. Again, I was scared. As badly as I want to look into your eyes again, I didn't want to see them cracked and overrun with pain because of me. So, forgive my coward move in apologizing this way. It's selfish, but it's the best I can do because I feel ashamed. I haven't slept well. I haven't been eating well. And I'm fucking up with my businesses. Karma, I guess. Well, I don't want to make this too long, but thank you for watching all the way through. I hope you can find it in your heart to forgive me."

Caleb's words painted a picture of a man filled with regret, who had faced his fears and come to a profound realization. I cried listening to his message. A hurricane of emotions swirled within me —pain, resentment, but also a glimmer of hope. Caleb's vulnerability touched a place deep within my wounded heart—the small part that wanted to heal. Despite everything, I couldn't deny something still felt special between us. Still, I had trust issues now.

As the video message ended, Caleb's voice lingered in the air, leaving me with a choice. I could choose to hold onto my pain and wariness, or I could choose to embrace the possibility of forgiveness and healing. Neither would be easy, and doubts still lingered, but Caleb had taken the first step toward reconciliation.

I closed my laptop. I needed time to think. Why did my life feel like a bowling ball constantly crashing into pins of emotions at full speed? The weight of deciding was heavy. I let hours go by until the evening turned to morning. I woke up to a text from Caleb that came through before I had figured out if I would ignore him or give him a chance.

Hey, Morgan. I'm sorry to bother you, but I see that my package was delivered yesterday. I hope you opened it. I'd do anything to hear from you, his text read.

His message was anxious. My eyes were still bleary with sleep as I read it again, fighting the urge to call him right away. With every passing second, I realized I didn't have the heart to ignore him. Everything between us had ended so abruptly that I wanted to hear more from him. I wanted to talk. Despite my negative feelings about it all, I thought it took a lot for him to bare his soul and plead for a second chance. And perhaps, just perhaps, I could try to open my heart once more. If he'd apologized any other way, I don't think I would have given in, but his admission and what I saw on screen broke through the unfinished walls I'd been building around my heart since he left. We were both flawed and scared, and I decided to reach back out and see if it were realistic to navigate our insecurities in different ways.

As I picked up my phone to call in that moment of vulnerability, doubts and trust issues blazed through me like a wildfire. *Can I believe him?* I wondered as the phone rang. *Can I trust that he won't run away again at the first sign of difficulty?*

"Morgan!" he answered excitedly.

Whether I was making a mistake or not, I'd reopened the door. "I got your package."

There was a moment of silence on the other end, as if Caleb were holding his breath. Then he spoke, his words filled with sincerity and determination. "Thank you for calling me. I understand if you're hesitant and unsure."

I remained silent.

Caleb rushed to fill it in. "I can't promise that everything will be easy, but I promise I'll be honest, the way you've known me to be. And I promise to go deeper with you if you let me. I don't want to lose you."

I listened to him, wishing I could be with him physically in the moment. "I'm nervous. I'm unsure. I could be making a huge mistake letting you back into my life—"

"You're not," he cut me off.

"But I never wanted to lose you either."

"I'm sorry."

"So . . . how do we do this?" I asked genuinely.

"By being together as much as we can so we can talk face to face. I can come see you today, if you'll have me."

As we continued our conversation, I felt a glimmer of hope rekindling within me. I remembered that sometimes the most difficult journeys could lead to the most beautiful destinations and hoped that would be true for us. Caleb drove almost three hours to see me that night.

CHAPTER 13

"I once read a quote that said, 'Healing comes from being, not doing,'" Caleb said in our hours-long conversation that night. He'd started apologizing with his eyes the moment he saw me, and then audibly in the elevator ride up. We talked and cried, shared and revealed new layers of ourselves. Once the kindling of an inkling I had to forgive him grew to a flame. Our conversation—once again—became fluid. "I never forgot that line, even though I read it years ago," he continued. "It was in a random social media post I'd seen from a conscious sexuality teacher named Jonti Searll, but it resonated with me deeply."

"Why?" I asked. I sat across from him in my living room.

He leaned forward. "Well, it forced me to think deeply. To be brutally honest with myself and force myself to feel the entire spectrum of human emotions instead of running from the painful ones. That's why I came back to you, Morgan."

"I'm not here to heal you," I protested.

"That's not what I meant."

"Because if there's one thing I know about myself by now, it's that I am not willing or able to heal grown men. I have my own emotional work to do. Even more so after the last month."

"And I'm sorry for my role in that." He perched further on the edge of his seat, nearly about to fall off, but respecting that I didn't go closer to him yet. "All I meant was I tried throwing myself into work when you weren't in the picture. I even got back in the fields to *do* more manual work instead of sitting still to *be*, feel, and process what was going on."

"I should have been out there to crack a whip on you!" It was a terrible response, but I didn't realize it until the words had already tumbled out of my mouth. Clearly, I was still pissed at him.

"And I would have let you. Maybe not in the field under the blazing sun, but in my dungeon, yes."

How did we get here again? I laughed. Something about the last part of our exchange cracked open a wild reservoir of emotions in me, and I cackled. "Fucking shit!" I threw a pillow at Caleb. "Damn it. I hate that I like you so much!" I confessed, a full smile painting itself onto my face.

"May I?" He gestured at the spot next to me, also grinning.

"Ugh. I guess."

He quickly came over to me, leaning into my space as much as he could. "You can hit me if you want. I deserve it. You can work out your pain in a controlled, passionate way if you need to. And I'm not trying to come off as a weirdo either."

"Well, you're not doing a great job," I jabbed.

"Look, I don't want us to be one of those couples with an 'it's complicated' status, but—"

"We're a couple?" My neck couldn't have swiveled back any faster.

"I would like to be."

"Whew, Caleb!" I threw my hands up. There he went again—a cargo train going full speed.

"Let me slow down. I just have a lot going on inside, and I want to get it out. I've missed you, Morgan. Yes, I want us to be a couple. No, I won't disappear on you like that again. And yes, if you need to put your hands on me to relieve your pain and the trauma I caused you, I'm willing to submit. I know this is all new to you, but I can explain if you decide you want to try. It may be therapeutic for both of us, honestly. I'm owning myself here, flaws and all, to get off to a fresh start with you. What do you say?"

I gave in and pulled him closer to me, not wanting to be dishonest about my hope for reconciliation. "I say yes," I answered consciously. "But this is your *only* second chance."

"I swear that's all I need!" He beamed and excitedly pulled me in for a kiss.

I didn't resist. I let go. I went with the flow, kissing him deeply. Passionately, until he leaned all the way back on the couch and I was on top of him. He tugged at my clothes to get them off while hungrily touching and squeezing me. My body writhed with pent up sensations. He moaned and I moaned. Our breathing hastened. We were all over each other, and soon just naked enough for Caleb and I had the kind of make-up sex that made tears fall from my eyes when I climaxed.

Two weeks later, after hours and hours of conversation repairing our relationship, I was heading back to Caleb's ranch. He said he'd created the safest space for me to explore and express myself in totality.

"Nothing will be as different or extreme as you might have imagined," he'd assured me when I confirmed I would spend the weekend with him.

I'd expressed to him in a previous conversation that despite him crushing my heart, I still found the thought of inflicting any real pain on him distressing because I still liked him—I held back on saying I loved him even thought I thought I did. He'd then asked me to describe what I kind of scenes I thought could happen in his playroom, and I did, giving the most cliché and extreme examples. The dark dominatrix. All black everything. Patent leather. Too-high heels. Whips. Chains. Cruelty. Yelling degrading and demeaning commands.

Caleb paused before responding. "It could be that. Yes, that's a style that some people like to perform. But that isn't *the* style."

I was confused.

"I want you to think of what you might want—only what *you* want—not what you think I desire. If you don't want to be mean to me, then don't. If you don't want to wear a costume—"

"I don't mind the heels," I'd jokingly interrupted.

"Then wear them," he'd smiled. "You see, a lot of people think that sex dungeons, BDSM and kinks in this area have to be one way. They don't. And for us and what I think we need to do to heal and keep moving forward, it needs to be more along the lines of navigating what you want from moment to moment, and me providing it. This is how we'll build trust and a stronger bond. We can graduate to heavy stuff later if you want to, but for now, it could be as simple as you ordering me to give you a two-hour foot massage while you read or watch a show."

I hadn't thought of it like that at all. "Hm."

"It could be you telling me to draw you a bubble bath and making sure the water never goes lukewarm. It could also be you sitting on the queening chair and making me eat your pussy until my tongue is worn out from exhaustion."

"Caleb!"

"Well! The point is you don't have to read my mind or follow any pre-written rules."

"What about pain?"

"What about it?"

"What if I do want to hurt you back, but I don't know how in this context."

"Keep it in the context of pain *play*. You aren't trying to go to jail, are you? How much pain are we talking?" He'd joked.

"Of course not!"

"We can cross that bridge when we get to it."

"Okay."

*What do **you** want?* The question echoed through my head as I was getting dressed and packed for the weekend. I wanted to feel strong. Powerful. In control of my emotions and actions. I also wanted to feel secure. I needed to feel trust between us. I replayed our last video chat in my mind as I pulled into his driveway. My heart pumped a bit harder than usual. Though we'd chat about formulaic attire, I still found myself dressed in all black except for wearing red, patent leather pumps. They made me feel sexier.

"Hello, gorgeous," Caleb opened the door looking and smelling like bliss.

I could have melted at his smile. "Hey," I whispered.

"Come on in," he stepped aside. His house was warmly lit, and soft music drifted throughout like a cool breeze. Contrast. There was always a contrast when it came to Caleb.

I stepped out of my heels and Caleb took my bag in one hand, and my hand in the other. He led me to the main living area. "That's new." A small canvas print on the bookshelf caught my eye. It read: *Life is about expansion, not restriction.*

"Yeah, I read it somewhere online, and it resonated with me, so I had it printed. I feel like I need to see it as a reminder," he said. "Want a drink?"

"Of course." I was eager to relax. The feel of his shag rug against my feet was a welcomed sensation.

Caleb brought over two highball drinks and pulled out a couple's card game called, *Better Together*. "I figured we could try something different this time."

This is why I can't quit this man, I thought. Caleb was always so thoughtful and unpredictable. He was fine. He could cook. Sex was explorative and fun. He was the kind of man I thought only existed in books.

We played the game for a while, answering all kinds of questions to reveal everything from where we'd most like to be kissed to what kind of trouble either of us would most likely get arrested for. It was amusing and completely put me at ease. Meanwhile, his playlist went from "Whipped Cream" by Ari Lennox to "I Want You" by Luke James. We played and we danced. We drank and we ate. We even had a moment of the most terrible karaoke I'd heard in my life, but I loved it. As time ticked on, we eventually landed in his bedroom. I told him that I wanted him to wash my body as if I were a goddess to be worshipped.

"At your service," he responded, and gently undressed me, guiding his warm hands across my skin as he unbuttoned my blouse and bra, unzipped my skirt, and pulled off my panties.

Caleb tended to me intentionally, so much so you'd have thought he was getting graded for the assignment. I lost myself in the firmness of his touch. His focus. He traced my jawline, my collarbones, my chin. . . he even added essential oils to the palms of his hands, so I could inhale the scent as he moved his hands in front of my face. My heartbeat quickened.

"Get on your knees," I ordered him, and he obeyed. I didn't have to give a follow-up instruction.

A sudden rush of craving ran through me when I felt his tongue lapping me up. My legs shook, but he held me in place. This wasn't like our first time, when he kissed everywhere but my clit to extend the session. Caleb dove into me greedily, licking, sucking, kissing, teasing until the wetness from my yoni flooded him with a nectar.

I moaned, feed him, gyrating, and rocking my body to feel every sensation of his lips, tongue and beard.

Caleb was all action. Intense. Fully absorbed in eating me out until I trembled and swayed. He had a way of humming while going down on me that created a warm and thunderous vibration. "Fuck! Oh, yes." I used one hand to brace myself on the wall and the other to grab a fist full of his hair. He moaned. I gasped. He whimpered.

Caleb smacked my ass, pulled it apart, pushed it back together, rubbed it and smacked it again, working me into a deep state of ecstasy. Eventually, he slowed down and gently rose to face me. He stared deeply into my eyes and his lips curved into a smile before asking, "How else can I serve you, Morgan?"

Well, damn. His words were like a song written just for me. I didn't have an immediate answer to his question, I was still floating in the deliciousness of our intimacy. Caleb wiped me down with a warm washcloth. He offered no words, only that penetrating gaze. He pulled me closer, wrapping his big arms around me and kissing my neck.

"Take me to your dungeon," I told him.

He bit me gently, as if my request opened his appetite for even more.

"And when we get down there, I want you to make sure I'm comfortably seated, then bring a few of your toys to me. Ones you think I'd enjoy exploring."

"Clothed or unclothed?" He'd had a towel wrapped around his waist.

"Naked," I responded quickly. I was starting to get the hang of it. A playful glee built inside me. This was fun! It was such a different dynamic and experience to solely think of what I wanted and ask for it.

When we got to his playroom, Caleb brought me a large feather, a pair of nipple clamps and what he called a "violet wand." It was a hand-held electrical stimulation device for sensation play.

"It's low-current," he explained, "and I think you might like it. "Don't let the electric part scare you. It's about as intense as finger-nails against skin on its lowest setting—otherwise, it's just a cool prop to make things more exciting. You'll love the glow and crackling energy it emits on my skin. Or yours..."

"Should we have a safe word?" I was part serious, part joking with my question.

"You're always safe with me, but it's good practice to have one anyway."

"Okay...what should it be?"

"You tell me, love!"

"I don't know!"

"Okay," he paused and thought for a moment. "How about Whiskey Sour?"

I cackled! I don't know what I was expecting him to say, but it wasn't that.

"You don't think that suits us?"

"I guess it does."

"I mean, we could always go with 'Yellow Crocs,' we know how much you love those."

"NO THANK YOU!" I smiled at the memory of our first meeting. "Whiskey Sour it is."

He grinned.

"Turn on the TV," I said. I felt like I needed something else to get me going since we'd broken the mood. "Do whatever you have to do to set a nice scene for me, please."

Caleb turned on porn that had women who actually looked like they enjoyed what was going on. "When you pay for it," he said, "you get better quality." I made a mental note. "Do you..." he hesitated.

"What?"

He bit his bottom lip, unsure of whatever he wanted to ask.

"What!?"

"Do you do edibles? Like, Delta 8 or THC?"

"I don't know what Delta 8 is, but yes, I've had weed gummies before. Why?"

"I mean, it can be a great way to reset the mood, if you want to indulge. You can have a tiny piece if it's been a while for you."

I debated it. *Say yes.* My inner voice pushed me like a dumbass teenage friend. "We can do that," I said. Why not? I trusted him and wanted to relax a bit more.

"Okay, cool! I have some that I know you'll love!" Caleb went to the kitchen and came back with a small plate of THC-Infused watermelon wedges and mango slices. I was expecting pieces of candy, not actual food. Of course, he would be extra with this.

"You just had weed fruit laying around?" I teased.

"Sort of. It's my wind down after a long day," he confessed. "Only these two have THC in them," he pointed. "The rest are regular. And you," he looked at me and smiled, "only eat half of one for now. They're light, so you'll still feel in control...just more relaxed."

I was excited at the thought and went for a piece of mango. Thirty minutes later, I was going up! All my inhibitions were gone. All my hesitance was gone. All my baby-step dominance showed up.

"Crawl to me and kiss my feet," I told him.

Caleb did as he was told. He also sucked my toes, massaged my arches and begged for more instructions.

"Look me in my eyes and repeat after me, 'I am yours to command.'"

"I am yours to command," he echoed.

I towered over him feeling more powerful than I ever had in my life. "Hold your position until I tell you to move." I circled him like a tigress circling her pray. I grazed his skin with my feet somehow instinctively knowing to place one on his chest. He exhaled heavily, loving it. "Beg for my touch." *Shiiit, I could get used to this!*

"Oh, Morgan..." I heard him "Please touch me...please...I want to feel you so bad..."

I glanced up to see two women with strap-ons pegging a man on tv. Another guy was in a corner stroking his dick while watching the threesome. This was a lot, but I loved it. "Get up," I told Caleb. The porn, and the weed, and the whiskey were sending me I started to touch myself as if I were in heat. *God damn!* Rubbing and bouncing my middle finger against my clit. My pussy was starting to drip and throb. Caleb started to caress his dick while watching me play with myself. He got himself pumped up and grabbed a bottle of lube to enhance his stroke. Our mutual masturbation was hot. We kept at it for a while until he asked if I wanted to try the wand.

I slowly nodded yes. "Be gentle."

"Of course." He sat me down on his sofa and slowly brought the want close to my sides.

I felt a slight tingle and liked it. "Mmm..." I watched as a thin violet light went from the wand to my skin and felt even more aroused.

"Is that a good intensity or do you want more?"

"It's good."

"Okay," he moved it from my sides to my breasts and slowly circled my nipples.

"Whew! Shit! Boy!" I heard my expression almost in slow motion with the cocktail of sensations I was feeling. "A little more intensity there," I told him. "Oh, my damn..." The feeling turned into a mild shock. Caleb pulled it back a bit without my asking him to, but either way it felt incredible.

"You like that?"

"Yes...yes," I spoke breathlessly.

He carefully stimulated me for a bit longer before I took the wand from him and told him to lay down so I could ride his face. I loved that. From there we coasted into a trance-like state of boundless pleasure. We took turns holding each other down, rolling around, kissing, licking, biting, scratching. We started and we stopped. We heightened the drama with his toys and props, from the feather to an anal plug. He didn't insert it in me, but I did let him rub it against my backdoor. He did stick his tongue in there though. It felt so fucking good that at one moment, I tossed my head back and mouthed "I'm in heaven. I'm in heaven. I'm. in heaven!!!"

From front to back and top to bottom, Caleb and I spent two days savoring each other. I even tied him up and had my way with him. It was so much feeling, discovering and bonding with each other. We *saw* each other in the midst of unleashing ourselves from expectations and specific end goals of sex. We had so much fun, and I felt so free, it was like I'd tasted hedonistic paradise. It wasn't often that I felt safe enough to explore and be curious. It was rare that I found myself in an environment that was judgement-free—even when I was alone because I tended to judge myself harder than others. It was unheard of for me to believe sex could feel connected to spirituality, but I felt that with Caleb—in a dungeon, of all places. It was way past physical. Our time felt equally spontaneous yet thoughtful. Caleb and I had several other moments of honest conversation.

"Thank you for forgiving me," he said. "I mean it. I never said I was perfect, even though I tried so hard to be that guy when we met."

"No one is," I admitted, and there was a pause in our talk.

"And thank you for being willing to try so many new things with me."

"I enjoyed it all. And I think you were right about it being good for me to use play to negotiate boundaries and scenes...to feel empowered."

"Oh, you're feeling powerful now?" He smiled.

"A little bit," I blushed.

We kept chatting, and again, he iterated that because of me, he learned that life was too short for meaningless connections. Our love making was in body, soul and mind. It was smooth, and down like perfectly aged whiskey.

END

ENJOYED THIS BOOK?

Please consider leaving a review on your favorite retailer site or shop.cherilnclarke.com to help others find something they might like too!

Find me on social media @cheril_nicole_ on Instagram and @cheril.n.clarke on TikTok.

OTHER BOOKS BY CHERIL N. CLARKE INCLUDE:

Rift: The Sensual Portal Series Book 2

Trip: The Sensual Portal Series Book 1

Trick or Treat: A Halloween Quickie

The Edge of Bliss

The Beautiful People: New Orleans

The Beautiful People: Las Vegas

The Beautiful People: New York

Losing Control

Spoken Word albums by Cheril N. Clarke (as C. Nicole):

Honey

Drip